DANDELION SUMMER

A Novel

TRICIA L. SANDERS

First edition. September 12, 2023.

Copyright © 2023 Tricia L. Sanders.

ISBN: 978-1962175012

Cover Design by GetCovers

DEDICATION

This book is dedicated to the amazing Chinwag Ladies. These ladies welcomed me into their group at a time when my spirits were lower than low. Chinwag is a British term for a chit-chat or gabfest and boy, do we gab. We also laugh and cry and share a ton of useful and sometimes useless information.

In no particular order the Chinwags: Rose Meyer, Rosario Gutierrez, Kirsten (Lambie) Lynch, Marilyn Dempster, Sher Louden, Roseanne Hyman, Marlene Palanca, Joan Henderson, Esmeralda Cortez, Connie Hasselbach, and Alexandra (Lexy) Lenz.

ACKNOWLEDGMENTS

All acknowledgements begin with my family, with whom all is possible.

To my readers for whom I write, thank you for allowing me into your homes, cozy reading nooks, and wherever else you dare to read.

Many thanks to my advance reader group - Meg Gustafson, Barb Schmidt, Lee Dunn, Jan Tomalis, Emmy McCabe, Kara Marks, Julie Lacombe, Mary Ingmire, Maggie Herrel, Dee Doub, and Amy Connolley.

To my editor Cayce Martinez at Kingsman Editing Services, thank you for riding herd over me and my words.

CHAPTER ONE

Determined to distract myself from waiting for the results of a recent round of tests, I dropped a pile of boxes on the floor outside my late husband's closet. After putting off the inevitable by taking far longer to assemble the boxes than necessary, I opened the door and entered. Nothing had changed in the past year and a half, not even the faint fragrance of his favorite cologne. I choked back a sob, grabbed a carton, and went to work.

Working slowly and methodically, I folded each of Michael's dress shirts, careful not to fold in wrinkles—as if packing for a trip rather than a ride to the local thrift shop. I moved on to his pants, checking each pocket for loose change, forgotten credit cards, or other reminders of him. Each time my fingers moved across an object, I winced.

Truth be told, I secretly hoped to discover a stray receipt to a local hotel, a phone number scribbled hastily on a bar napkin, or a love letter not written in my hand. Not that I had written any love letters in the last thirty years. Then I would have proof that Michael's distance and coldness were the result of an affair. I could live with that because then I could let go of my guilt. The guilt of knowing I was the one who ruined our marriage. If only I could blame his indifference on an affair, then I could stop being angry at myself. Stop holding our family together for the sake of our children. And finally let Michael go.

After taping the last box, I took one last look at the empty closet. High on the shelf, where Michael's athletic apparel had previously been, sat the urn that contained his ashes. It had started out on the living room mantel, but after seeing it every day, I'd finally moved it to his closet where I didn't have to be reminded.

I took it to the living room and returned it to the mantel.

Running a finger across the smooth porcelain vessel, I said, "What am I going to do with you?" In the months prior to his death, we had talked about his wish to be cremated, but the talk had never progressed to where he wanted his ashes spread.

"Surely you don't want to remain forever sitting on the mantel, being dusted once a week." I shook my head. *Stop it, Annie. Talking to this urn is why you moved it to the closet.* No, the urn would not stay forever on the mantel, but I didn't know just yet what to do with it. I could put it back in the closet and let the kids deal with it once I was gone, too, but somehow that didn't seem fair to them.

Tears welled in my eyes as I thought of all the things I should have said to Michael before he died. The answers I wanted but did not get. The possibility that my latest round of tests would reveal that I, too, had a fatal disease. Would we have a different ending if we'd had a different beginning?

Get yourself under control, Annie.

I took my phone and a glass of wine to the patio. I would think about his urn later. For better or worse, the view from my lounge chair was just as depressing as Michael's closet. Dandelions flourished amid the once-lush hibiscus, lantana, and coreopsis, all in serious need of deadheading and pruning. At some point—I couldn't remember when—I'd given up on caring. The weeds overtook my backyard, and I let them grow. It seemed too much a chore to dig up each one by hand, being careful not to uproot a neighboring plant or bush. Besides, the bees loved the yellow flowers. Maybe someday I'd make dandelion wine. Probably not.

The phone rang and I jolted. I scanned the display and saw Tim's name and number—Michael's best friend. My finger toyed with pressing the icon to answer, but instead, I let it go to voice mail. The irony of the call was not lost on me. I hadn't heard from Tim since Michael's memorial service a year and a half ago. Now today, of all days, he reached out. Too little, too late.

I met Michael and Tim my senior year at college. They were both third-year law students. Though they looked enough alike to be brothers, they were opposites in the personality department. Where Tim was outgoing and funny, Michael was introverted and brooding. I had mistaken the brooding as being thoughtful and driven. After several years of marriage, it was not so charming. Michael was often sullen and moody toward me. He hid that trait from our children, the public, and even Tim. But I felt it full force. He was still thoughtful and driven in his work and public life, but at home, the moodiness surrounded him like a dark cloud in a thunderstorm. When he wasn't interacting with the children, he holed up in his study until the wee hours of the morning, coming to bed only after I had long since fallen asleep.

My memories were interrupted when the phone rang again. Had I not been waiting for the doctor's office, I would have ignored it. A glance at the screen told me it was the call I had been dreading. My stomach clenched, and I hesitated before finally answering.

"Hello."

"Annie Chisholm, please." My doctor's voice sounded brisk and stern. Not at all sympathetic.

"This is Annie."

"Annie, it's Dr. Bench. Do you have a minute to go over your test results?"

I sucked in a breath, bracing myself for bad news. "Yes."

"Everything came back normal, except your cholesterol is a little high. And like I said when you were here last week, your blood pressure is borderline." She sighed. "I don't think it's anything that modifying your diet and staying active can't resolve."

I couldn't seem to let go of the air in my lungs. "That's it? All the tests are back?"

"Yes. I have everything. You can check your account online and see all the results, including some dietary suggestions. I'll want to see you back in six months to review your progress."

"I'm not dying?" I had bolstered myself for this conversation. Well, not this one. The one where she told me I was terminal.

She chuckled. "You sound disappointed."

"No. I j—I just thought with all the symptoms I'd been having, there was something dreadfully wrong. Are you sure? Do we need to retake the tests?"

"Blood pressure, my dear, and stress. How long's it been since Michael's death?"

"A year and a half. But—"

"But nothing. Annie, I've run every test imaginable in the last year, and there is nothing wrong that a little diet and exercise won't solve. If you're feeling anxious, I can prescribe something to help."

I pulled a stray thread from the hem of my shirt and rolled it between my thumb and forefinger. "No."

"Is there anything else I can do for you?" she asked, more empathetic this time.

"You are certain I'm not dying?"

"Annie, we're all dying. None of us can skirt death, but there is absolutely nothing in your chart to indicate that your death is imminent. Losing a spouse is traumatic. Have you been to grief counseling or seen a therapist?"

"No, that's not really my thing." Spilling my guts to someone was the last thing I wanted. There was too much baggage in my past to drag it out to a stranger.

"If you change your mind, I can make a referral," she said.

"No, I'm fine, really. This is great news. I was just prepared for the worst-case scenario."

"All right then. Can I transfer you to scheduling to get your follow-up appointment on the books?"

"No. I'll take care of it later." I forced a smile and vowed to reduce the stress in my life.

CHAPTER TWO

The vow lasted about an hour. My doorbell rang while I was rinsing my wine glass. Looking back, I should have ignored it. But no, what did I do?

I opened the door.

Tim's presence set off a range of emotions I hadn't begun to deal with. I assumed he'd slowly fade into the past—become a part of my history. He'd done a pretty good job of it since my husband's death. Michael and Tim, Tim and Michael, the two had been inseparable as long as I could remember, even before I could remember—long before we had become acquainted. They'd grown up together, gone to college together, even done a stint in the Peace Corps together.

My relationship with Tim? Well, that was complicated. While the three of us bonded immediately, Tim and I had formed a tighter connection. At least I had *thought* we had formed a tighter connection.

"Afternoon, Annie," he said like we were pals, like he hadn't disappeared from my life after Michael's service. His dark, rich tan angered me. Had he found a new golf partner since Michael's death? Life clearly hadn't stood still for him like it had for me.

"Tim," I said flatly. The feelings of abandonment returned. After Michael's service, Tim had left the church without a word. He hadn't even returned to my house where the ladies from church had taken over and prepared a meal. No calls the next day, the next week, or even the next month. Nothing—until today, a year and a half later.

"I owe you an apology." His eyes did not meet mine. "It hurt too much. Michael was like my brother. Hell, he was more like a brother than my biological brother."

I held up a hand. Before I could stop, the words rolled out. "I know. I know. The hurt is never-ending . . ." I blathered on like an idiot. Where bitterness had taken root, I found empathy springing forth like weeds. All the unkind things I'd imagined myself saying if I ever saw him again melted away. I reached out and took his hand.

He sighed and pulled me into a hug. "God, I've missed you. Missed Michael."

Patting his shoulder, I nodded. "It's been a rough time." But apparently not too rough. A sleek ivory and brown motor home the size of Texas, towing Tim's car, filled one side of my driveway. That spark of anger reignited. He'd only come to say goodbye.

I would have lingered in the hug. I needed to be close to someone. Michael and I hadn't shared many intimate moments since his diagnosis. There had been occasional pecks on the cheek and the perfunctory "I love yous," but our days of rosy romance had faded long before his diagnosis. We had faded into the background of his illness and our past. That's not to say we didn't love each other; we did. At least I loved him even with his flaws and hurts. I had always held out the hope of healing us, making us what we had once been. Held out for finding those six glorious years we had shared a lifetime ago.

Common sense pulled me away before I made a fool of myself. My entire life had started with Tim, and as if it hadn't felt like it ended a year and a half ago, the big beast in my driveway just proved that now it would. Or at least, it would end the life I'd built with him beside Michael and me as our best friend. It would be too easy to conjure a reason to stay in his embrace. He was hurting. I was numb. Nothing good could come from it.

"You're taking a vacation," I said, suddenly aware that my jeans were too snug, and my University of Florida sweatshirt had a stain of unknown origin.

"Can I come in? We need to talk."

Famous last words. I'd said the same words to my mother more than thirty-six ago when I told her I was pregnant. Ditto for the time my son dropped the bombshell that he intended to forgo college and "find himself" traveling the back roads of Europe. The same words Michael said to me two years ago when his doctor diagnosed an inoperable brain tumor.

I led Tim to the back of the house, not that he needed leading. He knew my home as well as I did. He and Michael had sweated and cursed over the blueprints—planning every nuance.

He pulled out a barstool while I busied myself making coffee. My hands trembled as I ground the beans. Had he sold the law practice and dumped the money into that monster sitting out front?

On the days when melancholy hadn't ruled my life, I had picked up the phone numerous times to call him. But each time, I resisted. He had turned his back on me. There was no Tim in my life before I met Michael, and there was no Tim in my life after Michael died. But damn him, I missed his presence. I missed his sense of humor. I missed him.

"You're selling the firm," I blurted out, more an accusation than a question.

"No. I've been considering it, but I wouldn't do that

without talking to you." He patted the seat next to his. "Come sit."

I poured his coffee, topped it with a spoonful of sugar and a splash of 2 percent, and placed the cup in front of him. The anger that had festered warred with the elation I felt at seeing him again. If I let anger win, I ran the risk of pushing him away. If I let elation win, I ran the risk of making a fool of myself. I settled on neutral. "You've got some explaining to do."

He grimaced. "I know. I've been a horrible friend. Michael would have been so disappointed."

"Michael?" I smirked. "What about me? I needed you. My oldest friend disappeared from my life with not even an inkling."

He dropped his head. "You're absolutely right. I don't know if I can explain it. At least not so it makes sense."

I stared at him. "Try."

After a ragged breath, he said, "When Michael died, it was like this chasm of grief opened up and swallowed me. The day of the service, every time I looked at you or Kaitlyn or Kyle, I sank deeper into that chasm. You had your family with all those memories of Michael. I felt like an outsider, standing outside the perfect family watching how stoically and perfectly you dealt with your grief while I wallowed in mine. The Chisholm family making everyone else feel better while they had lost their husband and father. I could not deal with that."

His words hit me hard. The facade that had been my life rose out of the depths to protect me like it had all those years since Michael had rejected me. Denying the unpleasant aspect of my life and turning on a bright, shiny smile for everyone, making everyone else feel good while I suffered—it had taken me years to perfect the image of perfect wife, perfect mother, perfect family. Michael and I were the only ones who knew it was hogwash.

There were times when I thought Tim had seen through our performance. Being Michael's closest friend, he had an insight into Michael that I had never been able to breech, but apparently, we were good at our roles. I had dropped the pretense after Michael's death by keeping to myself and disappearing from my social life. I couldn't stand to keep up the facade, so I hid.

If I wanted to get my friendship back on track with Tim, I needed to level with him. Tell him the truth about my life. But could I? I needed a clean slate and fresh start. I had lived this lie for so long, it felt like a part of my fabric. The only Annie I knew, and I wanted to separate myself from her.

"Do you still feel that way?" Tears built up behind my eyes, but I forced them back. I had missed him. I knew Kaitlyn had missed him. Kyle was almost a thousand miles away, so he'd returned to his life after Michael's death.

"No. That's why I took a chance and came over. I tried to call, but you didn't answer. Didn't return my call." Tim scrubbed a hand through his graying hair. "I assumed you were dealing with Michael's death in true Annie form, but Geneva mentioned you hadn't done the annual fundraiser for your women's group, and no one on the committee has seen you since Michael's death."

"I've been busy." The lie continued. Now was not the time to come clean. I wasn't strong enough to expose my weakness. He was leaving anyway.

Tim quirked an eyebrow.

Michael's former secretary, Geneva, and I had been friends for years. After Michael's death, I'd made excuse after excuse not to have lunch or go shopping or volunteer. "Did Geneva get her nose out of joint because I wouldn't co-chair the Junior League Cookbook Committee?"

"Don't blame her. She's worried about you," Tim said.

"I suppose."

"Can we call a reset and go back to normal?"

I wanted to laugh. The thought of going back to normal made me nauseous. "It will never be normal." Despite what Michael and I had or didn't have, I still missed him. I had held out hope that we'd find our way back. I couldn't turn my back on our years together like they had never existed.

"Of course. I totally understand. You'll find a new normal. It's taken me almost a year to find mine. It hasn't been easy." He perked up. "Speaking of finding your normal, I have something that might help."

Uh-oh, here it comes. My lips drew together in a disapproving smirk.

"Don't look so dubious."

"Does this have anything to do with the behemoth outside?"

Tim laughed, finally. "I've rehearsed this conversation in my head for a week, but I don't know any other way to say this than just to come out with it."

I topped our cups with fresh coffee.

Reaching into his pocket, he withdrew a key and slid it toward me. "It's yours. At least for the next six weeks."

Had he taken leave of his senses? "What's mine?"

"The behemoth, as you called it, is a Monroe, Model 34AJC, Class C Motor Home. Thirty-four feet of diesel-guzzling homeyness."

I pushed the key back. "Good joke. Now tell me the truth." Tim wasn't a prankster, at least not without being goaded into something by Michael, which obviously wasn't the case. Dead men didn't play practical jokes.

Sunlight cascaded through the kitchen window and glinted off Tim's glasses. He leaned back on the stool, and the light scattered across the countertop, highlighting the silvery flecks in the white granite. "I'm serious. Do you remember what today is?"

I didn't need to look at the calendar. The date was etched in my mind. Michael had promised me a vacation for as long as I could remember. He never took the time while he was growing the practice, nor did he have time once he had.

"One of these days, Annie," he'd always say. "We'll go anywhere you want."

I had counted on that being our time to reconnect—to move forward and heal our marriage. But I'd stopped asking, and he'd stopped promising.

"Michael's retirement date," I said. "Fat lot of good it did him." Fat lot of good it did me. I'd hung on to the thread of promise forever. Every year telling myself it would be the last year I spent waiting to reconnect with Michael Chisholm. Every year, telling myself I'd give it one more year.

Tim picked up the key and held it between his thumb and forefinger. "This is the key to the promise Michael made. The vacation you've always wanted. I know he stunk at taking time away from the firm. He told me how much you wanted to travel and how much you enjoyed the trips you took before we started building the firm. And I encouraged him to take time off. I swear I did. But you know how stubborn he was.

"Now you have the opportunity to get away. It's too late for him, but it's not too late for you. It's your future, Annie. Find your new normal. Michael's been gone a year and a half, and you're in the same rut."

"I'm not in a rut," I lied. But if walking around in a fog, staring at four walls, wasn't a rut, what was?

"How often do you get this kind of chance handed to you? I have friends who would jump at the opportunity."

Not that I would admit it, but the idea of a trip anywhere was music to my ears. A small tingle traveled the length of my spine, but I ignored it. "You're my savior? Did you come back to whisk me away and fulfill Michael's promise?" I pointed to the key. "Where were you when I needed a shoulder to cry on or when I couldn't start the lawn mower? You were his best friend, and you disappeared. Now you want to take me on vacation. I'll pass." I pushed off the stool and took my cup to the sink. My eyes burned from the hot sting of tears. I blinked several times.

Tim's arm went around me. "I'm sorry, Annie. I am so sorry."

His aftershave enveloped me, and I swayed, clutching the sink to keep from toppling over.

He ripped a paper towel from the roll and handed it to me. "Come back and sit."

I stiffened. He put his arm around my shoulder and urged me toward the stool. I dabbed at my eyes and followed. When I was seated, he took both my hands in his. "I'm not going. It's your trip."

"I don't understand."

Tim released his grip and raked a hand through his hair. "Where do I start?"

I frowned.

"When Michael found out he was dying, he asked me, no, he begged me to help him plan your trip. I knew about his promise, of course. But after his diagnosis, he knew he'd never make the trip. One afternoon we were talking, and he had this idea of giving you the vacation as a gift."

"I'm supposed to take out of here for parts unknown driving that thing by myself? Not going to happen."

Tim headed for the living room. "Don't go anywhere," he called over his shoulder. "I'll be right back."

Don't go anywhere. Ha! I eyed the bag of chocolate next to the refrigerator and considered heading for my bedroom with it. If I acted now, I could lock the front door and bury myself beneath my blanket. Only I didn't move. It was as if my feet were two huge bricks. A sitting duck in my own kitchen, waiting for the double-barreled shotgun blast.

He returned with a manila envelope. "This will explain everything. Six weeks of road-hugging adventure to collect your thoughts. Maybe try your hand at writing again. I can't imagine that you don't miss it. Writing was such an important part of your life way back when."

I eyed the chocolate again, but it was too late. "What is this?" I took the envelope. It was thick and lumpy. Michael's handwriting caught my attention, and my stomach lurched. Since his death, I'd come across other things with his handwriting, and my gut always had the same reaction. He was dead, but it was always one more reminder of the person he'd been. The Michael whose *M*s were twice as big as the rest of his letters, the *I*'s he forgot to dot, and the slanted left-hand scrawl that would have earned him a ruler across the knuckles at any respectable Catholic school.

"It's a video from Michael." A smile spread across Tim's face. "It would do you good, Annie. Your new normal, remember?"

If he says new normal one more time, I might clobber him. "And you'd know because . . ." I remembered all the evenings after Michael stopped working that Tim would stop by and the two would sequester themselves in the den, presumably talking business. Toward the end, Michael could barely put together a coherent sentence, but like faithful friends were, Tim always was there for him.

"Because he needed my help to make it. And then"—he waved his hand to the front of the house—"to make the arrangements for the RV."

I placed the envelope on the counter. "Nice, but I have other things to do. I'm too old to take off driving across the country. Besides, I can barely back my car out of the driveway without running over a mailbox. There's no way I'd be able to navigate that thing."

Tim's shoulders drooped. "You have to. For Michael. It meant everything to him. Besides, I don't remember you being afraid to tow his parents' camper that you guys used to borrow every summer before . . . Sorry," he said.

I closed my eyes and swallowed hard, pushing memories back into cobwebby corners. "No."

"Then there's the writing. Have you even given that a thought?"

"Not going to happen. I need to be here for Kaitlyn. She's been struggling since Michael died." The truth was she was struggling before Michael died. Life was a struggle for my daughter, and it didn't help that I babied her. She popped in constantly, usually looking for a meal, a dog sitter, or a laundress, and I begrudgingly obliged. Cooking and laundry gave me something to do. Besides, she was about the only human contact I had other than going to the store once or twice a week. But it suited me, didn't it?

With her job as a barista, she had free time to spare when she wasn't at the gym. So much for a year and a half of college. Me leaving might force her to grow up. It might give her the added incentive to find a more permanent job and do her own chores.

Tim glanced at his watch. "Think about it, Annie. That's all I ask. There's a tablet in the package with a video. Watch it. I'll leave the key. Go look. It's a beaut. Everything you need for a road trip. The fridge is full of easy-to-fix meals. I even stocked it with your favorite wine. All you have to do is move in your clothes and personal items."

"No—" He was out the door before I could finish my sentence. I didn't chase him out. Instead, I watched from the porch as he unhooked his car and drove away.

CHAPTER THREE

The Monroe, Model 34AJC, Class C Motor Home beckoned from the driveway. I'd never seen the inside of an actual you-drive-it RV, and curiosity gnawed at me. This was a huge leap from the overgrown aluminum bullet we'd borrowed from my in-laws back in the day. One peek couldn't hurt. After I satisfied my curiosity, I'd return the key to Tim.

After he left, I'd thrown the key on top of the envelope. I picked it up and cupped it in my hand. Just as quickly, I dropped it and covered it with the envelope. *This is nonsense.* There was no harm in looking.

A gentle breeze ruffled the leaves of the trees lining the western side of my driveway. The RV's brown and beige swirls seemed to undulate as slivers of sunshine danced down its length. As I approached, the immensity of the RV dwarfed me in comparison to the car I usually drove. I imagined myself lumbering down the highway with a WIDE-LOAD sign plastered to the front bumper, holding my breath every time I crossed a bridge.

In my wildest dreams, I'd never imagined a vacation on the road by myself. Michael and I had done that as newly-weds. In retirement, I had dreamed of moonlit evenings in

Tuscany, sunny skies and aquamarine oceans in the Caribbean, or maybe even gloomy days stowed away in a London pub knocking down mugs of dark, frothy ale. Those were my retirement dreams—not maneuvering a tank through an obstacle course.

I shivered as I turned the key in the lock. The memories of the crowded trailer we'd pulled behind my father-in-law's Suburban overwhelmed me.

Vacations at the beach, splashing in the ocean, and eating platters of shrimp drenched in butter. Making love under the stars with the warm kiss of the ocean lapping at our toes. I could almost hear the gulls and the melodious sounds of a child's laughter. I leaned against the RV, gulped in deep breaths, and rubbed my eyes hard, shaking away the memories.

When they faded, I straightened, squared my shoulders, and climbed aboard. Tim had extended the RV to its full width by pushing out expandable walls. Two enormous captain's chairs, covered in mocha-colored leather, faced the windshield. I deposited myself in the driver's seat and swiveled around to take in the rest of the space. A matching sofa and banquette took up one side of the living/dining room with a center walkway. The opposite side contained a kitchen area complete with sink, small stove, microwave, and a full-size refrigerator. The décor looked straight out of a home design magazine—no expense spared. Every inch of space was utilized from the overhead cabinets to the small pantry, even a flat-screen TV. This beauty was a far cry from the 1980s tow-behind.

Another memory surfaced. A hot, humid night sitting by a campfire, swatting mosquitos, and drinking cold beers to celebrate Michael's decision to open a law firm with his best friend. Michael and I whooped and hollered and danced around the fire, a little too drunk for our own good.

Later that night Kyle and Kaitlyn were conceived. Little

did I know it would be our last camping trip. I shook my head and stood, tucking away my past and focusing on the here and now.

True to his word, Tim had stocked the refrigerator and cabinets with a full complement of groceries, wine, and even chocolate. I helped myself to a foil-wrapped square of deliciousness. A small bathroom occupied a nook between the living area and the bedroom. I continued my trek and feasted my eyes on the bedroom.

What in the world had gotten into me? Drooling over a motor home I had no intention of using.

"Nice try, Michael," I said. I wasn't sure what had motivated him to think an RV trip would make up for everything that had gone wrong in our marriage. I was happy being home in my element, wasn't I? Did I really need six weeks on the road to cure everything that ailed me?

No, this old girl belonged at home, tucked in her own bed, not gallivanting around the country in an overgrown breadbox on wheels.

By the time I made it back into my kitchen, tears streamed down my face. Damn Tim for showing up. Damn Michael for dying. Damn me for caring. I threw the key on the counter, grabbed a handful of chocolate, poured myself a glass of wine, and scurried to the patio.

That's where my daughter found me. Of course, I had knocked down a few more glasses of wine, and I had even gone back to the RV to retrieve the box of expensive chocolate Tim had provided.

Kaitlyn's eyebrows shot up when she saw me. "Have you got company?"

"Nope, just me and the dandelions." I referred to the noxious yellow blooms sprouting all over my yard. The damn weeds seemed to have a mind of their own. One would shrivel and die while three appeared in its place. My yard looked like a *before* photo for *Better Homes and Gardens*.

She wrinkled her nose, plopped onto a lounger next to me, and kicked off her shoes. "Did you know there's a huge RV in your driveway?"

"Yep." I took another chocolate and bit into it, savoring the creamy smoothness as it melted. "You want one?"

She glanced at the box. "Whoa, you sprang for the good stuff, but no thanks. I just came from the gym." She didn't say it, but I knew she thought I should get off my butt and follow her lead. And truth be told, I probably should.

Besides working as a barista, Kaitlyn lived at the gym. Her life consisted of hot yoga, selling overpriced coffee, and complaining that she had no money. "Are you planning a trip you didn't tell me about?"

"That's your uncle Tim's project," I said around a mouthful of chocolate. "He thinks I should chuck all my responsibilities and hit the road in that tin can."

"You heard from him?"

"Yep, the first time he contacts me since Dad died, and he comes by with a plan for me to take a vacation. Nervy!"

Kaitlyn laughed and slapped her knee so hard, she left a red mark.

"What's so funny?"

"You driving that thing. Seriously, Mom." She burst into a fit of giggles.

"I'll have you know—" I stopped. She knew very little about me before she and Kyle came along. The first six years of my married life, I kept bottled up like a rare wine. Those memories were locked away. It hurt too much to bring them out in the open. This morning in the RV had brought some of them to the surface.

"What?" She craned her neck and stared at me.

"Huh?"

"You'll have me know what?"

I shrugged. "I could do it. It would take practice."

"Are you serious?" Kaitlyn sobered. "I don't want to hurt

your feelings, but aren't you a little old to be traipsing around the country by yourself? What if you had a heart attack or a stroke? Besides, I need you here."

"Kaitlyn, just stop. There's no need to get insulting. I'm barely eligible for AARP. Lots of people my age take up RVing." It didn't take much to trigger my anger these days, and she didn't deserve my ire. It's not like I had even given serious thought to taking off in the thing. "You want something to drink?"

"No, but don't let me stop you," she said too patronizingly for my liking. Her cell phone buzzed, and she snatched it out of her pocket. "I need to take this. I'll be right back." She headed into the house, and I tipped my wine glass and drained it.

A text alert sounded on my phone.

TIM: HAVE YOU GIVEN IT SOME THOUGHT?

I ignored the text. He wasn't the only one who could ignore a friend. It was a passive-aggressive move, but between him showing up out of the blue, Kaitlyn insinuating that I was old, and the cursed dandelions, I was ready to throw an old-fashioned hissy fit. Was I too old to throw a hissy fit?

"Too old. Ha!" I couldn't do a thing about Tim and probably could not change Kaitlyn's mind, but, glaring at the dandelions, I vowed payback. If I had to dig up the suckers by hand, they would die. Busy plotting my revenge, I didn't hear Kaitlyn return.

"Mom, can we talk?"

Uh-oh. Those words again. Twice in one day could be nothing but an omen.

"I'm not discussing this with you. It was Tim's idea, not mine. Forget about it. I'm not going anywhere."

"Mom, it's not that. This is serious."

"Dear God, don't tell me you're pregnant," I said. My

daughter could barely hold a job. She'd never be able to take on a baby.

She blew her nose and sniffled. I sat straight, my mind reeling with possibilities. "What is it, Katie?"

"Can I move back home? My lease is due for renewal Monday, and the landlord is raising my rent. I already can't afford it, but now . . ." Kaitlyn plunged her hand into the box of chocolate.

There it was. I exhaled the breath I'd been holding. Part of me wanted to scold her for blowing off college. Her second year, she got it in her head that if no degree was good enough for her twin brother, it was good enough for her. A view I did not share, but what could I do. It's not like I could force her to go to school and make good grades. Well, maybe I might have forced her to stay, but I'd learned with Kyle that Michael wouldn't back me up. So, against my wishes, she quit.

Maybe this was a gift dropped in my lap. I had been looking for the opportunity to get her to give school another chance. "Well, I don't know."

"Mom." Kaitlyn's mouth drew into a tight frown. "This is my home too. If you don't let me, I'll be sleeping in my car." Her eyes narrowed. "Or I might move to St. Louis with Kyle."

I slapped my hand over my heart. "You'll give me a coronary with your threats." My worst nightmare involved Kaitlyn moving away, but I would never let that slip. As far as Kyle was concerned, I might as well have been on another planet. When it came to work, he was his father's son.

"You said you were too young for a heart attack." Katie threw a piece of chocolate at me. "I'm moving back. Get used to it."

If my plan had any chance of working, she'd need to squirm a bit before I relented. She was right, it was her home. If I had the ability to help, I'd never deny my children anything. But I wasn't above letting them dangle a bit. "Not so fast, sister. Last time I checked, my name was on the deed. Annabelle Chisholm. Not yours and not Kyle's. Your father and I worked hard to provide a roof over your head. Unless you know something I don't know, whether or not you move in is my decision." While I hadn't had a paying job the whole time Kyle and Kaitlyn were growing up, I'd worked hard keeping the house livable and the family fed.

"But . . ."

"No buts. Now scoot and let me think about it."

Kaitlyn's lip curled into a pout. "I only have until Monday, you know."

I pointed to the door. "Out! I'll call you with my decision."

"You need to think about getting out more," Kaitlyn said over her shoulder on the way out. "You're getting crabby."

CHAPTER FOUR

The more I thought about Kaitlyn moving back, the more I resented the idea. I'd grown fond of my seclusion. Having a thirty-year-old underfoot would put an end to my quiet evenings. Not to mention I could hardly enforce curfew, and I didn't know if I could tolerate her coming in at all hours. My sleeping patterns were erratic enough without her upsetting them even more.

Though, if I let her come home, I might gain leverage to get her back in school. I could easily foot her tuition—that wasn't a problem. With her living here, she could concentrate on her studies and still hold down her job to pay for incidentals. If I could put up with her until she finished her degree, it could be a win-win for both of us. She'd get an education, and I'd get a daughter ready to face the adult world and stand on her own two feet. Her major complaint about going to college had been that she didn't know what she wanted to do. Maybe now she could figure it out.

Kyle had intended to work toward a bio-medical engineering degree, but after "he found himself" in Europe, he got a job selling appliances at a big box store. He parlayed that position into store manager, then regional manager.

Kaitlyn never followed in his footsteps when it came to luck. Her poor choices slapped her around at every opportunity. She'd tried hard to be independent, but every step forward, something knocked her two steps back. Last month it had been tires for her car after I'd noticed her driving around with barely any tread. The month before that, the electric company threatened to cut off her power because her bill was late—for the fourth time. The only reason she hadn't lost her gym membership was because she worked ten hours a week on the front desk in exchange for gym privileges.

Sleep did not come that evening. I tossed and turned, going over everything that had happened that day. From boxing up Michael's clothes, to Tim showing up with a far-fetched notion that I needed to travel in an RV, to Kaitlyn yet again needing Mom to come to the rescue. Despite all of it, Tim's suggestion about writing niggled at my brain.

I punched the pillow and turned over, but my mind would not quiet. What would I write? Did I have a novel in me? Articles? A sad commentary on widowed life after a lackluster marriage? My mind drifted into the land of what-ifs. What if Michael and I had never married? Would I be a freelance journalist heading to far-off places on assignment? I sobered at that thought. Kyle and Kaitlyn meant the world to me, so that line of thinking was irrelevant.

Then I thought about Tim. I had dated Tim before Michael and I wound up together. In fact, Tim was responsible for me and Michael having our first date. Not a real date, but a substitute date. Tim and I were supposed to go to the Barrister's Ball. At the last minute, Tim was called home. His mother was gravely ill. Rather than disappoint me by missing the ball, he roped Michael into taking me. Maybe it was because the night was so magical or because I was a bit tipsy, but I fell hard for Michael and he for me. When Tim returned to school, weeks after his mother's funeral, he stepped aside and never once tried to intervene. Never once. It had hurt that

Tim hadn't fought to get me back, hadn't pounded Michael into the ground for stealing me away. Nope, he just acted like it was perfectly normal for me and Michael to be together.

I threw off the covers and padded to my study, formerly Michael's study, and opened my laptop, hoping inspiration would come. The flashing cursor mocked me. How was I at a loss for words? When I worked as a reporter, I could pound out a story without thinking. Inspiration sat on my shoulder. Between the caffeine high and the high I got from accomplishing a story, my mind never lacked a word or phrase. Now I drew a blank.

I picked up my phone, telling myself that a quick game of solitaire would help percolate ideas. Three games later I was no closer to a story than I had been when I was tossing and turning in bed. I scrolled through my contacts, and the first phone number I came to was Abigail Lawson. We used to play tennis and meet for coffee—before Michael died. We could talk for hours, and she always knew what to say when I was feeling down. If one of our kids had acted out, Abigail and I commiserated, reminding the other that kids were not always perfect. Oh, and we always shared stories of our husband's latest quirks that irritated us to no end. She never knew the full extent of my relationship with Michael because that was tampered down and hidden from view.

"Hello." Abigail's voice was groggy from sleep.

"Oh my goodness. Did I wake you?" That was a stupid question. I glanced at the digital readout on my laptop and saw it was nearing midnight. What was I thinking?

"Who is this?"

"I'm so sorry. I didn't realize how late it was."

"Annie, is that you? Jeez, it's the middle of the night. Why are you calling now? We haven't talked in over a year. What's going on?"

"Nothing. I—I thought. Never mind, I'm sorry. Please forgive me."

"It's nothing, Fred. Go back to sleep," she said to her husband. "Have you been drinking?" she asked, her voice louder again. Her tone bore no resemblance to the bubbly woman who always had a smile and kind word for everyone.

"N-no, sorry. I didn't realize the time, is all." I gently pressed the disconnect button. Talk about stupid things to do. This one kind of set the precedent. Hopefully, Abigail would be discreet and not spread my flagrant faux pas to the neighborhood gossips. Nothing like getting the tongues wagging that I'd finally lost my mind.

Now that I'd thought about it, most of my friends—no, all of them, really—had stopped coming around. And if I examined the cause seriously, it was me.

I scrolled through the contacts and tried to determine the last time I'd seen or heard from each person. Other than relatives, it had been over a year for everyone. I still received Christmas cards from many on the list, addressed only to me. But in turn, I'd not mailed any out. What did that say about me? Too wrapped up in myself to give a simple greeting to a friend.

Why did I think calling Abigail would solve my dilemma? She hadn't said it aloud, but her accusatory tone hit home with the message that I hadn't bothered to return her calls after Michael died. Or in the months since. She'd finally stopped calling.

I slammed the laptop closed, grabbed an afghan and a glass of wine, and went to the patio. Maybe the stars would inspire me. Or maybe I'd fall asleep to the sounds of crickets and night bugs.

CHAPTER FIVE

I woke to the sound of the phone ringing and waited for Michael to answer it, until I realized I had been dreaming, and Michael would not be answering the phone. I was still on the lounge chair on my patio and the phone was in my lap. Glancing at the screen, I recognized the St. Louis number and groaned. Kyle never called. If he said we needed to talk, I'd hang up.

I swallowed the dryness in my throat and sat up. "Hello."

"What's this about you taking a road trip by yourself? Have you lost your mind? Do you know what could happen to a woman your age out on the highway?" Kyle's voice boomed. "Not to mention the fact that you've never driven an RV before."

"I see you've talked to your sister."

"She said Uncle Tim had something to do with your wild idea. I called him, but it went to voice mail."

"Take a breath, Kyle." My son tended to rant until his asthma kicked in.

"You can't be considering this."

"What if I am? I'm not ready for the nursing home. I still

have a few good miles in me." I covered the phone in case he heard me giggle.

"Kaitlyn said you've been acting odd."

"Odd?"

"Yes, she said you told her you had to think about it when she asked to move home."

"Back off, Kyle. Her living situation is between me and her." I wanted to tell him about my plan for his sister, but with the way he was acting, he'd just call her and spoil the whole thing. "If she calls you again, you can tell her that. Her living situation is my decision, not yours."

"Who are you?"

"I'm your mother, and it's time I started acting like it." I disconnected before I lost my temper and said something I didn't mean.

Kyle intentionally pushed my buttons. Everything he did, he did to get a reaction. And it usually resulted in me giving in to whatever catastrophe he'd cooked up. Michael had checked out early on and left me to deal with Kyle's temper tantrums. Michael was a family man when the show was necessary. Over the years, I'd learned the best way to deal with my son was not to deal at all. Kind of like a volcano. Just get out of the way and let him blow. Once he settled down from whatever tantrum he was having, peace returned. My mistake had always been letting the tantrum get out of hand.

I made myself a strong cup of coffee and went to the bathroom to shower and change. When I looked in the mirror, I barely recognized myself. Huge shadows lay beneath my eyes, and my hair stuck up in odd angles, frizzed from the early-morning humidity.

Kyle's words echoed in my head.

"Who are you?" I said to my reflection. And that was a damn good question. Who was I? Who was Annie Chisholm?

I thought about the answer as I showered and washed my hair. More than half of my life I'd spent being a wife and mother. There had to be more to my legacy than that. Who was I as a person? Apparently not a good friend since I'd pretty much abandoned my friendships. But those weren't the important parts of Annie Chisholm. When the mother, wife, and friend titles were removed, who was Annie Chisholm, and what would she be remembered for?

Who was I before being a wife and mother? Maybe in finding that person, I would find me. With that thought in mind, I dressed quickly, applied makeup that I hadn't used in ages, carefully styled my hair, and decided to do something I hadn't done in years.

"One salted caramel mocha," the server said, setting my drink on the table.

I thanked her and opened my laptop. If I was going to find Annie Chisholm, it would start with writing. Thinking a coffee shop would get me away from the distractions of home, I had packed up my laptop, a notepad, and a pen. Now I stared at the screen like it was an alien. A brief idea flitted through my head, and I jotted it on my notepad. Just as quickly, another idea surfaced. I wrote it down too.

"Annie. Annie Chisholm, is that you?"

I looked up and saw a smartly dressed woman headed my way.

"Oh, my goodness. I can't believe my good fortune," she said.

I stared, trying to place a name to her face, but drew a blank.

"Are you by yourself? Do you mind if I join you?"

Bewilderment must have shown on my face. "Uh, I guess so."

She extended her hand as she slid into a chair. "Belinda.

Remember? Belinda Baldwin. From our days on the *Chronicle*."

I did remember. How could I forget Belinda—the woman most likely to become . . . fill in the blank with any successful-sounding noun. We had interned together at the *Chronicle* three summers in a row. When we graduated, Belinda was hired as a copy editor, and I'd been hired as a reporter. From there Belinda's career blew up. She quickly climbed the corporate ladder. Last I heard, she'd gone on to work for the parent company in New York.

Suddenly all the makeup and hair fixing I'd done this morning made me feel dowdy and unkempt. Belinda looked every bit the corporate mogul. Her hair was styled and fell loosely at her shoulders. Her suit screamed Florida casual, yet businesslike: an ecru linen summer pantsuit with a hot-pink silk blouse underneath. A single gold chain with an opal encircled her neck. Matching earrings dangled from her earlobes.

I wanted to rewind my day and still be sitting on my patio, but I reached across the table and shook her hand. "Of course I do."

"I'm so sorry about Michael."

"Thank you." I searched my mind, trying to remember if she'd sent a card. I'd received so many, it was hard to keep track.

"I sent a card," she said like she'd walked right beside me and my thoughts all day. "I'm sorry I didn't make it to the memorial service." Belinda called the server over and ordered a chai latte. "You want a muffin to go along with your drink?"

I shook my head. "I'm good."

"Don't be silly. Their morning glory muffins are the best." She ignored me and ordered two heated and with extra butter. "We have to treat ourselves once in a while."

"I suppose you're right. Thanks."

She eyed my laptop. "What are you working on?"

Belinda and I had sat in this very shop too many times to count years ago before coffee shops were trendy. Back then it was a bakery with a few tables squeezed in. We'd meet here before work for apple fritters and coffee to commiserate about our intern positions and speculate if we'd be hired when we graduated. Both of us were full of hopes for long and illustrious careers.

"Nothing really. Just brainstorming." I closed the laptop and scooted it aside. The brainstorming so far had resulted in a few ideas worth considering.

The server arrived with muffins and Belinda's latte.

"Don't tell me you're working for the *Chronicle* again." She pushed one of the muffins in front of me.

I had to admit it look amazing and smelled like heaven. "No, just kicking around some ideas." I pinched off a piece of muffin, smearing it generously with butter.

"Remember our morning bakery trips and how we'd bounce ideas off one another, hoping to find an attention-grabbing story that would assure the newspaper we were worth retaining?"

I laughed. "I do. It was a good time back then."

"Have you read the drivel that's being published these days? Some of those headlines, I can't even . . ."

"I know what you mean," I agreed. "You'd think the least they could do is use spellcheck."

We both laughed. Conversation with Belinda was so easy. It was like we'd picked up where we left off. This was exactly what I had needed last night when I was scrolling through my contact list. The idea ran through my head to bounce my ideas off Belinda. Maybe my creative juices would return. I shrugged it off. She had more important things to do.

"Oh Annie, how I've missed you. We should do this more often."

"Aren't you still in New York?"

"No, I split with them a couple of months ago. Took an

early retirement, and I'm in the process of starting a women's lifestyle magazine. I'm back in Florida on a house-hunting trip. My mom is having some health issues, so I need to be close by."

"I'm sorry to hear about your mother. I just assumed you were here on vacation. I never dreamed you'd move back. The magazine sounds amazing. That's the ultimate dream to be your own boss doing what you love."

Her phone rang, and she glanced at the screen. "Excuse me a minute. I need to take this." She went outside to take the call.

I let my mind drift to the possibility of having someone to bounce ideas off. A friend to meet up with for coffee and conversation. For the first time in a long time, I felt a spark of joy. Sure, I loved Kaitlyn and I looked forward to her visits, but this was different. I had always felt a connection to Belinda when we worked together, like we had been sisters separated at birth. She was single and vibrant with dreams that I shared. When our internships turned into real jobs at the paper, we'd slowly drifted apart. She was still single, and her free time was spent barhopping and enjoying a bachelorette social life. Mine was spent doing laundry, making supper, and changing baby diapers.

"Sorry for the interruption," she said when she returned. "That was my real estate agent. He has a house that he says I have to see before it gets snatched up. Let's do this again." She pulled a small silver case from her purse and handed me a business card. "This has my cell number. Give me yours, and I'll put it in my phone."

I gave her my number, and she was gone just as quickly as she had appeared.

CHAPTER SIX

My eyes had barely closed when a summer storm rattled the windows. I pulled the pillow over my head and sank beneath the covers, my mood worsening as lightning created a strobe effect in the room. My chance meeting with Belinda had been such a highlight until I returned home and began dissecting our conversation. She'd seemed eager to reconnect. Maybe eager wasn't the correct word. Not opposed to reconnecting was more like it. Did we even have anything in common now? Was it too soon to call her? I dismissed that idea. She was a successful businesswoman. I was—who was I? That nagging question again.

The trash truck rumbled down the street, reminding me I hadn't set out the garbage bin. Last week, I'd forgotten, and now rank odors emanated from my garage. I couldn't live another week with the smell. I threw off the sheet, grabbed my robe, and made a beeline to the garage. The rain had slowed to a few sprinkles, and I arrived at the curb just as the truck pulled up.

"Classy ride ya got there." A burly guy in grimy coveralls hefted my trash into the hopper.

The RV. How could I forget? It took up a large chunk of

my driveway. Thank goodness Michael had insisted on a three-car garage when we built or else I would have never gotten my car out with this monster squatting on two-thirds of the space.

"Where ya headed?" He gave the bin a shake.

"Nowhere. It belongs to a friend," I said.

"Too bad. Thing like that could give you a whole new outlook. No worries, just miles and miles of open road. Me and the wife got plans to travel when I retire. If I ever get to retire. Bet your friend is looking forward to riding the road in style."

I shrugged.

"Lucky schmuck, your friend. I'd give my left nu—arm to drive down the road in that thing. My wife would think she'd died and gone to heaven."

A gust of wind carried the scent of rotting garbage.

"What's a thing like that cost anyway? Bet it cost a small fortune." He stared wistfully at the RV.

"Umm, can I have my bin back?" I hadn't had breakfast, and the smell of rotting garbage had killed my appetite.

He slammed it down in a puddle, splashing my robe. "Grouchy this morning, ain't ya? Just trying to make conversation."

Before I could respond, he climbed back in his truck and shifted into gear. On the way back to the garage, I grabbed the newspaper from my front porch and stuck out my tongue at the Monroe Model whatever-the-hell it was.

After starting a load of laundry, I wandered to the patio with a cup of coffee and the paper. The rain had come to a halt, and the sun peeked through the clouds. An air of dampness lingered, but a cool breeze seemed determined to break through the humidity. The dandelions mocked me in the gentle breeze. "We're here," they seemed to say, swaying in unison.

I unfolded the newspaper, took one look at the loosely

worded headline, and set it aside. Belinda was right. Where were the journalists today or at least the copy editors? I looked at the headline again and read the story—twice. First as a reporter and second as a copy editor. In my head, I rewrote the headline a dozen times. Each time better and punchier than the first. If hadn't lost my ability to suss out an attention-grabbing headline, maybe I still had the creative chops to develop a great story. That hope zipped through my head as I thought about the story ideas I had started while sitting at the coffee shop yesterday. Could writing a novel be much different from developing a great news story? More thought analysis, perhaps. An outline. A beginning, middle, and an ending.

Lost in my thoughts, I jumped when the phone rang. The display showed a number I didn't recognize.

"Hello," I said, bracing for a robocall.

"Annie? It's Belinda. Did I catch you at a bad time?"

I relaxed, trying not to give away the excitement I felt at hearing her voice. Maybe she'd want to meet for coffee again. "No, sitting on my patio."

"I've got a crazy idea that I'd like to run by you." She giggled like a schoolgirl.

I sat up and swiveled on the chaise to plant my feet on the patio. From the sound of her voice, it was more exciting than meeting for a cup of coffee. "I'm all ears."

"You know I told you about this magazine start-up. Well, after we met yesterday, I started thinking about how immense this challenge is and, well . . ." She paused.

"Yes." I hated when people got to the good part and stopped. "What is it?"

"I know it sounds nuts, but would you be interested in writing an article for the premiere issue? And perhaps a monthly column after that. I'd love to work with you again. It would be like old times except we wouldn't be working for the man."

"Are you serious?"

"Of course. I trust you, Annie. You had great instincts back when we were at the paper. You always came up with a fresh angle for every story you wrote."

A wave of panic shuddered through me, followed by a shiver of excitement. "Me? No way. I haven't written anything more exciting than grocery lists and excuse notes for school in years."

"Then it's time you got back to writing the good stuff. Take some time and think about it. In the meantime, I'll send you a little about my vision for the magazine."

Feeling more energized than I had in years, I gave Belinda my email address and disconnected. So energized, in fact, that I changed into old comfy clothes and began weeding the garden beds surrounding the patio.

A memory of weeding my mother's flower beds surfaced. How I'd hated it when she enlisted, no forced, me out of bed on Saturday mornings to dig weeds. I'd usually give the chore a half-hearted attempt, snapping off the weeds at ground level. Then she'd come out with her disapproving frown and the weeding tool I'd left on the kitchen counter. "Now, dig out the roots," she'd say.

Hours later, exhausted and sweaty, I reared back onto my heels, perspiration dripping off me like I'd taken a dunk in the pool. One last dandelion remained.

"You're mine!" I stabbed the digger tool into the dirt, attacking the root of the plant.

My garden looked like it had been attacked by a herd of armadillos, but at least the weeds were gone. A little work with a hoe and some mulch, and my garden would be as good as new. My road to a new Annie would take a bit longer.

CHAPTER SEVEN

After reading Belinda's vision for the magazine, I had an epiphany while showering. I really wanted the opportunity to write again, but to do that, I needed a break. I needed a break from staring at the same four walls I'd stared at every day since Michael's death. I needed a change in routine, a reason to wake up every morning. I needed to restart my stagnant life.

Yesterday I'd been sure that a trip was not in the cards for me. I stared out the front window at the RV still sitting in the drive, and an idea took root.

"Waddya say we take a trip, Michael," I said to the urn.

I could barely contain myself as I waited for Belinda to answer her phone.

"I hope you're calling with good news," Belinda said.

"I am. Or at least I hope you think so." I filled Belinda in on my idea to write a piece about saying goodbye to Michael by visiting some of the places where we had vacationed early in our marriage. "I hope you don't think it's too downbeat," I said.

"No, it sounds like a great idea." Her voice didn't hold the excitement I had hoped for. "It's just that I don't have that kind of money budgeted for a project like you're talking about."

"I have a—" Was I really considering taking the RV? The old Annie in me, the one who took chances and leaped before looking, screamed yes. The current Annie, the one who had squashed her dreams, screamed no. If I wanted to channel the old Annie, I had to leap. I took a deep breath. "I have a solution if you're still interested."

"Go on."

I explained the situation with the RV. Not everything. Not that it was my dead husband's idea delivered by his best friend, but the fact that I had access to an RV for the next several weeks and would be taking the trip anyway. Whew! I was doing this. Wasn't I?

After Belinda signed off on my idea with a hefty fee for the article, the old Annie kicked in and the self-doubting began. Could my earliest memories of Michael and me together change my outlook? Could they change me?

Regardless of the troubles we'd experienced, I loved him. We'd just drifted apart. No matter how much I'd blamed him, it was my fault too. I could have bridged the distance if I'd wanted. It just took too much effort. Once I had married Michael, I tucked my dreams into the closet along with my wedding dress and size ten jeans. Life happened all around me, but I didn't make it happen. I sat back and watched. The more time that went by, the easier it was to ignore the problems. Look the other way. Turn the other cheek. Retreat into myself.

Before I totally chickened out, I had to cement my plan or else I'd call Belinda and tell her I'd changed my mind.

CHAPTER EIGHT

My next task involved dealing with Kaitlyn and her living arrangements. I'd never doubted that I'd let her move back in. To that end, I'd even stripped her bed and put on fresh sheets, dusted, vacuumed, and made room in the closet. The dresser contained old clothes that she'd left behind. I packed them into boxes and made a pile for the local thrift shop. Once her room was habitable, I called and invited her to dinner.

I'd just pulled the lasagna from the oven when she barreled through the front door. Petey, her black lab, bounded into the kitchen and promptly stuck his nose in my crotch. I shooed him away with my foot. "Get away from me. If I drop this lasagna, you'll be doing time in the pound where Kaitlyn found you."

Kaitlyn kneeled and scratched him behind the ears. "Don't listen to her, Petey. She loves you more than she loves me."

"Go wash your hands and set the table."

While Kaitlyn gathered plates and utensils, I cut the lasagna into squares and slipped Petey a scrap or three. He gobbled them down and, being the traitor that he was, sidled closer and begged for more.

"I saw that," Kaitlyn said. "You can be gruff and mean all you want, but Petey and I know you're a softy."

More like a soft touch. No good deed went unpunished. I'd be giving up my privacy when she moved back home, and in return, I'd get a house full of dog hair and a slobbery patio door.

———

After Kaitlyn dried and put the last dish away, I poured two glasses of wine and followed her to the patio. The setting sun cast a rosy glow through the clouds in the west. Earlier in the day, we'd had a shower, typical for Florida, but oddly enough the humidity was nonexistent—the perfect evening for sipping wine and revealing my plan.

Petey had cornered a lizard underneath the lantana. His barking soon gave way to serious digging, dirt flying in every direction. This was what I had to look forward to. I should have had him dig up the dandelions instead of me.

"Pete!" I yelled. "Stop it!" For just a second, he stopped, then turned and looked at me. "No more digging." He cocked his head and sat down at the edge of the patio, continuing to watch the lizard. "Good boy."

"I wish he listened to me like that." Katie pulled her hair back and fastened it into a low ponytail at the nape of her neck.

"I got my bluff in early. He knows you're not serious. There's no consequence if he doesn't mind you."

"You think so?" she asked.

I nodded. Just like my kids when they were growing up— and now, for that matter. Michael didn't even have to try. He gave them a stern look and they toed the line. I couldn't ever recall Michael raising his voice to the kids. It had taken me a few years after they were born to get the parenting thing down pat, but I managed pretty good until Kyle's decision to go to Europe. That was when I had to admit my little ones had become adults.

"I've been thinking about your living situation, and I have a proposition to make. But hear me out before you say anything." Suddenly, I felt like a conniver. When Kaitlyn and Kyle were young, I never used bribes to get them to do what I wanted. Instead, I'd taught them about consequences. The mothers in our neighborhood play group used rewards to exact the behavior they wanted. Several times I'd witnessed a child totally out of control and a harried mother begging the little one to calm down and promising the moon or usually ice cream or candy.

I wanted my kids to behave because they knew it was the right thing to do, not because they would get a treat. Now that they were grown, I guess I still expected them to do the right thing. I'd hoped that by making this offer to Kaitlyn, she'd see the bigger picture and not see it as a bribe. I wanted to think of it as an opportunity since she'd already lived the consequence of dropping out of college.

"Why is it that I think I'm not going to like your proposition." Kaitlyn topped off our wine and leaned forward, elbows on her knees and chin resting in her hands. She had her father's inquisitive eyes.

"You don't have to accept it. You can always go running to your brother. *Again*." I had told myself I wouldn't mention Kyle, but she'd no more want to live with him than I would. I might as well put the option out there for her to consider.

Her cheeks turned pink. "He called you?"

"He did. Got downright self-righteous with me." Petey resumed his barking. I rose from my chair. "That does it." I grabbed his collar and walked him to the kitchen. "Now you have to stay in the house, while we sit outside." I closed the screen door and returned to my chair. Petey whined, but eventually, he curled up on the tile so close to the door, his nose pressed against the screen.

"Sorry, but when you started talking about taking off by yourself, I got worried. And I was mad because you acted like you had to think about whether to let me come home. Without thinking, I called him. Do you forgive me?" Kaitlyn looked down, not meeting my eyes—her repentant face.

I waved my hand in the air. "Don't worry about it. I can handle your brother. Been doing it for thirty years. He's a bag of hot air. If he blows long enough, he'll eventually cool off."

Kaitlyn giggled and sank back in her chair. "What's your proposition?"

"You know I'd never let you sleep in your car *or* move in with your brother for that matter." I laughed. "I cleaned your room, changed the sheets, and got it ready for you."

"Ah, Mom." Kaitlyn wrapped her arms around my neck and kissed me on the cheek. "You're the best."

When she pulled away, I shot her a stern look. "But you have to do something for me. Two somethings. One, I want you to go back to school."

Kaitlyn groaned. "Mother, I don't have the money for my rent, much less tuition. I'm barely making it."

I waggled a finger in her direction. "Exactly my point. If you go back to school, I'll pay your tuition. I still have the money that Dad and I set aside for you. You can keep working at the café for spending money."

"There's nothing that remotely interests me. I love working at the café and don't need a degree to do that. What would I major in?"

Shrugging, I took a sip of wine. "What does it matter? You'd have plenty of time to figure it out. In the meantime, you'd be doing something meaningful with your life. Who knows, you might get a degree in hospitality or decide to become an event planner and open your own business. There are tons of professions you'd be good at, but you'll never know if you don't try."

A smile tugged at the corner of her mouth. "Event planner sounds cool. I love parties."

Petey whined at the door and nudged the screen with his snout.

"Think he's learned his lesson?" Kaitlyn asked.

"Probably not, but let him out. That lizard is probably four houses away by now."

As if he knew he'd been a bad dog, he hightailed to where I sat, licked my hand, and lay down at my feet, never once acting like he cared about the lizard.

Kaitlyn rolled her eyes heavenward. "I don't know who's worse, you or him."

"See," I said. "It's all about consequence." Petey rolled over, and I scratched his tummy. I never said anything about not rewarding the dog. He moaned, and his back leg quivered when I found his tickle spot.

"What's the other thing you want me to do in exchange for moving home?"

There was still time to change my mind, but once I said it aloud to Kaitlyn, I couldn't. I didn't want her to get the idea that she could change her mind about going back to school. I had to set the example. I gulped, measured my words, and let them rip. "Since you're going to be here anyway, you can house-sit."

CHAPTER NINE

The next couple of days flew by. Between the driving lessons I'd badgered a neighbor into giving me, packing everything I'd need for the next six weeks, and talking Kaitlyn into not calling her brother, I had my hands full.

Kaitlyn made me promise to text. I didn't mind. Being on the road did not make me uncomfortable, but anything could happen, and it was good to know she was looking out for me. When I'd taught my kids consequences, I'd learned the meaning too. Not telling Kyle meant I didn't have to deal with whatever he wanted to dish out. I'd gone as far as threatening Kaitlyn with eviction and maybe even tar and feathering if she breathed a word of my trip to her brother.

I'd learned that I couldn't tow my car behind the RV, but Michael's Jeep was perfect. I sold his car soon after his death but couldn't stand the thought of parting with the Jeep that he'd babied. It still sat in my garage covered with a tarp. I arranged to have it serviced and had Tim show me how to hitch it to the RV.

Belinda and I had met for coffee twice to go over my proposal, and she'd given me her full approval. The only thing left to do was get on the road.

The morning I backed the Monroe, Model 34AJC, Class C Motor Home out of the driveway, Kaitlyn and Tim stood on the porch waving at me—Petey at their side wagging his tail. I said a silent prayer for my backyard garden and all the lizards that lived within. It took me two tries and asking my across-the-street neighbor to move the car parked at the curb in front of her house, but I finally got the motor home backed out of my driveway, and Tim gave me one more lesson on hitching the Jeep. Kaitlyn gave me a thumbs-up and nervously twirled a strand of hair around her finger as I drove away.

The knot that had grown in my stomach over the last couple of days slowly unwound the closer I inched to the highway. The RV, Monroe as I had dubbed it, had a three-month trial subscription for satellite radio. I'd found an oldies station, and I set it to music from the seventies and eighties. I turned onto the interstate just as Tina Turner launched into "Proud Mary."

Michael's video was safely tucked in an overhead cabinet and his urn strapped into the seat beside mine. Several times since Tim dropped off the RV, I'd considered watching the video, but I didn't want it to influence my decision. This was a decision I had to come to on my own. Michael had planted the seed, and now I needed to do it for myself. Not for him. Not for my kids. And not for Tim. I'd finally decided to take the video with me and watch it when I was well into my trip.

Though the trip to Atlanta was straightforward, I'd programmed my first destination into my phone's GPS. Driving through Atlanta always proved to be a challenge, what with constant road construction and frequent traffic-snarling accidents. Driving thirty-four feet of unfamiliar metal and towing the Jeep added to the test. I'd left early enough to beat the evening rush hour, but Atlanta was always a gamble.

The only reservation I'd made for the trip was at a small

campground on the outskirts of Nashville, but it wasn't for another two nights. It was the one destination where I knew I'd have trouble getting a spot to park the RV.

By the time I reached the outskirts of Atlanta, I felt strangely comfortable behind the wheel, but the traffic had increased, and my fuel tank was low. I should have filled up sooner and vowed not to make that mistake again. I didn't look forward to maneuvering Monroe through the streets of Atlanta in search of fuel. I sucked in a breath and decided to take a chance on waiting until after I had exited the city.

Changing lanes proved to be problematic. I had practiced back home, but always when traffic was light. My experience towing my in-laws' camper had not prepared me for driving this monster. The couple of times I'd gathered the courage to go around a slowpoke, I felt sure I'd cut the vehicle off. I hadn't heard the crunch of metal or seen cars in my rearview mirror hurtling end over end into the median. I took it as a good sign. Unless there was nothing but clear road behind me for twenty miles, I mostly stayed in the slow lane, doing the speed limit. Let the speed demons pass me. My hurry quotient hovered in the idle zone. After all, I was on vacation. A working vacation, but a vacation. The first one I'd had in over thirty years.

I maneuvered through downtown Atlanta and came out the other side feeling good. I looked like a giant turtle lumbering down the highway, but it didn't matter. With the city behind me, I found a truck stop and pulled up next to a pump. I hadn't realized how much fuel Monroe would suck down. After what seemed like forever, I went inside and purchased a soft drink and a snack.

The attendant, an older gentleman with a toothpick dangling from the side of his mouth, smirked. "Who's driving that rig you're in?"

"What?" I looked behind me to make sure he wasn't talking to someone else.

"Who's driving your rig?" he repeated.

I started to say that I was, but his attitude stopped me. "What difference does it make?"

"I didn't see anyone else. Driving a rig like that is man's work." He worked the toothpick to the opposite side of his mouth.

"Is that so?"

He hitched his pants over his generous belly. "Yes, ma'am, it is. The fairer sex can't anticipate all the hazards that come up when handling a rig that size."

I rolled my eyes and took the bait. "Okay, I give. Like what?"

He removed the toothpick and leaned over the counter. "Such as air pressure. You want me to come take a look?" He winked.

I slid my credit card into the machine and returned it to my purse. "I can assure you I have everything under control." Even if I didn't, I wouldn't tell him.

The door opened, and a scrawny guy in bib overalls entered. I took the opportunity and grabbed my drink and snack from the counter.

"Hey Jimmy," the man said to the newcomer. "This here fair damsel is driving that rig out there. Don't that beat all you ever seen. She don't look like she's got the oomph to steer that thing, does she?"

I froze mid-step, wanting to turn around and give the guy a piece of my mind.

"Shut your trap, Gus," the scrawny guy said. "Why you gotta harass all the ladies?" He held the door open for me. "You have yourself a nice day, ma'am, and ignore that old windbag."

I thanked him and scurried back to the RV, vowing not to stop here on my return trip. By the time I had strapped myself into the driver's seat, a light rain had begun falling. I turned back toward the highway and was met with a huge detour sign. The entrance ramp was blocked. I followed a line of cars and turned at the detour sign. The rain came down harder with lightning streaking across the sky.

My jaunt driving around town at home in Monroe had not prepared me for driving in the pouring rain on a narrow back road following a line of slow-moving cars. The road veered sharply to the left, and I soon lost sight of the highway. My insides gurgled as I fought the wind to keep Monroe on the road.

"This is all your fault," I said to the urn beside me. "If I ever get out of this, I'm turning this thing around. Screw your vacation."

An orange sign ahead assured me I was still following the route of the detour, so that made me feel a bit better. At least I wasn't lost. I tightened my grip on the wheel. The two-lane road seemed especially narrow, and the dotted center line faded into the wet blacktop. The farther I drove, the more the traffic thinned. I was now following a semi that I was certain was in search of the highway. A few miles farther, he made a left turn onto another blacktop. I turned, too, hoping against hope that I had made the right decision. A car behind me turned also, so I felt better about it.

My shoulders and hands ached from gripping the steering wheel. Sheets of rain pelted the windshield, and my wipers had a hard time keeping up. I didn't dare take my hands off the wheel to glance at my GPS for fear I'd run Monroe right into a ditch.

"If you weren't dead, I'd kill you myself for getting me into this mess," I said to the urn again. Clearly, I had lost my mind since I was talking to an urnful of ashes and driving in blinding rain down a country road with no shoulders and little to no visibility.

When the semi's turn signal came on, I breathed a sigh of relief, until I realized it was turning in to a driveway. Now what? I continued to drive, praying for another detour sign or something to indicate my whereabouts. The rain let up a bit, and I saw a church ahead. I turned on the gravel lane and drove into the empty parking lot. I turned off Monroe's engine and slumped against the steering wheel.

Tears welled in my eyes. I let myself have a good cry, vowing to never ever do something so stupid again. I was running a conversation through my head, trying to figure out how to tell Belinda that I would not be doing the article when I heard a rap on the door. I jerked upright and noticed a pickup parked in front of the RV with a young woman in the passenger seat.

"Hello," a voice called from outside. "Are you in need of help? I'm John Gaston, the pastor here at Grace United."

I stumbled over myself getting to the door. "Yes," I said as I flung the door open. "I'm lost. Terribly lost. The highway was closed, and somehow I lost the detour I'd been following."

The rain picked up, and the pastor held his hands above his head, shielding himself from the rain.

"Oh my, come in out of the rain." I motioned for him to enter the RV. He turned and flashed the woman in the truck the okay sign.

"Whew!" He climbed the steps. "We haven't had rain like this in months. The crops here are sure needing it. Now where you headed?"

I thought for a minute. "Home. To Florida. I need to get back to the interstate."

"Oh my, you are a bit out of your way, but nothing I can't help you with. Do you have a cell phone?"

I nodded and retrieved the phone.

He programmed my GPS and handed me the phone. "You shouldn't have any trouble, but if you do, give me a call." He pulled a business card from his pocket. "You're lucky you weren't here a couple of months ago. Our cell service was terrible, but we recently got a new tower, and we are five bars all the way."

I thanked him and watched as he ran through the rain to his truck. He fired up the engine but waited until I had pulled Monroe onto the road before he left. I said a silent prayer and headed toward the highway.

It took thirty-five minutes to reach the highway, but when I did, I did not hesitate. I turned south and headed home. Knowing I had a long drive ahead of me, I pulled off at the first rest stop and asked directions to the closest campground or motel.

—

After checking in, I found my camping spot and set about getting ready for the evening. The RV had walls that slid outward, making the living room and bedroom bigger. Tim had shown me the buttons that operated the moving walls, and I'd practiced a time or two. There was also a laminated copy of the setup instructions. The flip side showed all the details for locking down the RV and getting ready for the road.

I would have preferred a motel, but the campground was closest, and I just wanted out of the driver's seat. Too tired to think about hooking up the beast, I unfolded a lounge chair and sat outside with a glass of wine. What had started as a great day quickly turned miserable. I needed a minute to regroup, decide how to tell Belinda that I had second thoughts about the project, and possibly come up with an alternative that I could write from home. Yes! An alternative would soften the blow.

Quitter! I shrugged. Story of my life. Story of my marriage. When the going got tough, I gave up. What kind of lesson would that teach Kaitlyn? I was finally hopeful that she'd find some sort of footing instead of taking the easy way out. And what was I doing? The very thing I didn't want for her.

I closed my eyes.

"Hello, neighbor." Someone jostled my foot.

I jerked awake and screamed. A grizzled old man stood at the foot of my chaise.

"Holy heck," he said. "I didn't mean to scare you. Just thought you might want to get inside before the skeeters attack you."

"Jeez!" I leaped from the chair, barely missing the wine glass that had slipped from my hand. "What do you want? Who are you? You scared the crap out of me."

He held his hands in front of him. "Calm down, lady. I mean no harm. Me and the missus are next door. Saw you sitting here and realized you'd fallen asleep. It's almost six, and the skeeters will start biting. Don't want you gettin' eat up."

I glanced at my watch. "Damn!" How long had I been asleep? I grabbed the setup instructions, ignoring the little man.

He watched as I fumbled with the hoses and connections. I scratched my head, trying to clear the cobwebs from my nap. All the words on the paper blurred together.

"You need some help?" he asked.

I whirled around. "No. I do not need your help. I do not need anyone's help. What? Do I look like a helpless female who needs a man to take care of her?"

"Whoa! Calm down, lady. Just trying to be neighborly. Looked like you'd had a rough day. Pardon me all to hell and back." He turned and hurried back to his RV.

Well, that was certainly uncalled for. What was wrong with me? "Hey," I called after him. "I'm sorry. My day has been one catastrophe after another, and I took it out on you."

He kept walking.

Crap! I threw the laminated sheet on the ground, stepped into the RV, and went to bed on the sofa. I wasn't sure if I could use the toilet since I hadn't hooked up any connections, so if I had to pee in the middle of the night, I'd go to the woods.

CHAPTER TEN

My bladder woke me as the sun was rising. I had changed my mind about peeing in the woods and wound through the cramped RV to the bathroom. I'd suffer the consequences when I got home and had to clean the thing out. The thought of getting back in the driver's seat sent a quiver through me. Maybe after breakfast. I thought I'd seen a café when I checked yesterday.

I slipped into a pair of shoes and set out to explore. Several campsites were occupied, and judging by the lawn decorations and potted flowers, many of the occupants were long-term. Tall pines lined both sides of the campground entrance. I found the café with a Closed sign in the window. It didn't open for another hour.

A gravel path near the main entrance wandered to the left and I followed. Overhead, birds flitted from branch to branch. After the rain, everything smelled fresh and earthy, and the landscape was green and lush.

The gravel abruptly ended near a small stream where I found several picnic tables arranged in a grove of trees. I sat for a while enjoying the sounds of nature, wishing I'd had the forethought to bring a book. Instead, I found myself watching an older man and woman fishing. Both had perched on camp-stools, their fishing lines dangling in the water. Their laughter drifted to where I sat. I watched with interest as he baited her hook, and she reached over and swatted at his sleeve.

When she got a nibble on her line, she squealed with delight. He helped her land her catch, took the fish from her hook, and placed it in a bucket at his side. Then he bent and planted a tender kiss on her cheek. A tinge of regret filled me. Was that what it was supposed to be like to grow old with your spouse at your side? What did it take to keep those fires burning after all their years together? Could this have been Michael and me if we'd kept those fires burning?

"Hey there," the man hollered and waved.

It was the man from last night. Embarrassed by my outburst, I rose to leave.

"Hey, don't run off," he said. "We got off on the wrong foot yesterday, and I need to make it right."

"What did you do now?" the woman scolded him.

I waited until they caught up. "No, that's entirely on me. I'm afraid I snapped at your husband for no reason other than I had a crappy day. He was just trying to be nice, and I let my emotions get in the way."

The old man smiled. "I should have minded my own business, instead of butting in."

"Let it be, Calvin. You're always digging yourself in deeper than you need to," the woman said. I noticed that she walked with a slight limp.

"Can we start over? We're the Bittners. This is Betsy," he said, nodding to the pink-cheeked woman at his side. "I'm Calvin, but everyone calls me Cal." He reminded me of a deflated Santa. He stood no more than five feet, with a slight build. A full head of curly white hair, ruddy face framed with bushy eyebrows, and a full beard and twinkling blue eyes rounded out the picture.

"I'm Annie," I said. "Annie Chisholm."

As slim as Cal was, Betsy was well-rounded with an ample bosom. She stood a few inches taller than him and wore her salt-and-pepper hair in a fat braid that trailed down her back. I could picture her in an apron, flour dusting her cheeks while grandchildren waited for cookies fresh from the oven.

"Morning, Annie Chisholm. Pleased to make your acquaintance." Cal wore a funny hat covered in fishhooks and feathery lures. He shifted the bucket he carried and extended a free hand. "What brings you to these parts?"

Good question. Truthfully, I didn't know, myself, and telling him I was running away from a vacation with my dead husband in the seat next to me would probably send him and Betsy running for the hills. "Just passing through."

He tilted his head as if pondering my answer. He lifted the bucket of fish. "Me and the missus caught more than we can eat ourselves. How 'bout you and your mister joining us for supper tonight? Bets can fry a mess of these fishes along with some hushpuppies and taters, and we'll have ourselves a feast."

I hesitated. What would they think of a woman traveling alone?

"Now, Cal." Betsy put a hand on his arm and shook her head. "Trouble with him is he's never met a stranger. He's really quite harmless."

Cal chuckled. "Woman, you wouldn't know harmless if it bit you on the behind." He playfully patted her backside. "How 'bout it, Annie? These fishes are fresh as they come. Right, Bets?"

"Cal, don't be pushy. Annie don't know us from Adam," Betsy said.

"Well . . ." Fresh fish sounded good. But hopefully tonight I'd be eating at home in my kitchen.

"I'm wearing her down." He winked and tipped his hat. "I'm telling ya, Betsy is a genius with cornmeal and cooking oil. Did I tell you that her chocolate cream pie won first place at the Tennessee State Fair?"

"First place, huh? I'd hate to refuse dinner cooked by the Tennessee State Fair chocolate cream pie winner, but as soon as I get some breakfast, I'll be heading out."

"What? Why, you just got here. What's your rush?" Cal asked.

Betsy cuffed him on the shoulder. "You nosy old coot. Leave her be."

"But you didn't even get to see the sunrise this morning. Those clouds are supposed to move out later today, and it's going to be a glorious day. How about breakfast?"

"Cal," Betsy warned.

"Hush up. The lady said she was going to eat breakfast."

I chuckled. "Just waiting for the café to open."

Betsy hiked an eyebrow. "You waiting for that mess to open, you're going to be here awhile. They closed up last week, and no one has seen hide nor hair of them. Heard they filed for bankruptcy."

"Oh, well. I can pick something up on the road."

"Nonsense." Betsy linked her arm through mine. "What kind of neighbors would we be if we let you get on the road without a hearty breakfast."

Calvin nodded. "And we might even convince you to stay a day or two and see what God's country has to offer. Once you see the sunrise and nature's creatures beginning to stir, it will put a smile on your face. Not only that, but Betsy makes the best biscuits and gravy you'll ever put in your mouth."

I had to admit they drove a hard bargain, and my stomach growled and gurgled like I hadn't fed it in three days. "Okay, you twisted my arm. But then I'm getting on the road."

"Grab your mister and come on over," Cal said as we approached the RVs.

"I-I'm traveling alone. It's just me." That was harder to admit than I thought it would be. Letting my guard down forced me to come to a tough conclusion. I was alone. Sure, I had the kids, but they'd eventually get married and have their own families. Kyle had already made the break when he moved to St. Louis. Even though Kaitlyn had moved back in, it was only a matter of time before she'd find her footing.

"You're not one of them de-vor-sees, are ya?" Cal asked.

Betsy's eyes flashed with anger. "Well, Calvin Bittner, I never. You have no manners at all."

"A man has a right to know who he's inviting into his home, don't he?"

"I-I'm a widow." The words caught in my mouth, and it dawned on me that this was the first time I'd referred to myself as a widow. In the time since Michael's death, I still thought of myself as his wife. "I lost my husband last year."

Betsy cuffed Cal on the arm. "Now look what you've done. You apologize to Annie right this minute for being nosy."

"No apology necessary," I said. "Cal's right. You can't be too careful these days. I tell that to my daughter all the time."

A look of relief crossed Cal's face, and he turned to Betsy. "I ain't in the doghouse, am I?"

"Old man, you're always in the doghouse. Now let's get them fish home before Annie passes out from starvation." They were so cute together, just the right amount of sass and teasing.

When we arrived back at the RVs, Cal said, "Bet that rig set you back."

"Calvin Bittner, I swear. There you go again, poking your nose where it don't belong. You take them fish to the pavilion and clean them while I get breakfast cooking."

"It's okay," I said. "I'm only leasing it for a few weeks."

Cal grinned, took the bucket, and headed off down the lane whistling a tune.

"Men," Betsy said.

At eight sharp, I crossed the grassy area between our campsites. The smell of sausage greeted me. My stomach growled in anticipation. My cheese-and-cracker dinner was just a memory. Betsy carried a tray covered with a towel and placed it on the picnic table she'd set.

"Hope you like orange juice." I held out my contribution for breakfast.

Betsy grinned. "Our favorite."

I set the pitcher on the table. "What can I do?"

"Just sit. You're company." She scooted a plate of biscuits in front of me and called over her shoulder, "Calvin, Annie's here. Come on before breakfast gets cold. Bring that gravy I left on the stove and use a hot pad."

The table had been set with three pink-and-aqua-striped plates, a pair of salt and pepper shakers shaped like flamingos, pink tumblers, and aqua-handled utensils. I poured a generous amount of juice into the tumblers.

Calvin placed a skillet of gravy in the center of the table. He pulled a bandanna from the pouch of his overalls and tied it around his neck like a bib. "Let's eat." Calvin stuck his fork into a biscuit.

Betsy slapped his hand with a ladle. "Grace first, then we eat."

Between mouthfuls, Cal said, "I noticed you never got around to setting up your RV last night. Must have been cramped in there with those slides in."

Betsy gave him a death stare.

I choked on a bite of biscuit. "Uh, yeah. After the day I had, I just wanted to go to sleep."

Cal took a swig of juice and wiped his mouth with the bandanna. "Is this your first time out?"

My cheeks heated up. I nodded. "I guess it shows."

"Nothing to be embarrassed about. Why, me and Betsy, first time we took our rig out, it was a disaster."

Betsy laughed. "Only because he was too stubborn to ask for help. He got the lines mixed up, and he flooded the place. I was ready to call it quits before we even spent the first night." Betsy leaned close. "Is that what's happening with you, hon?"

Oh, how I wanted to disappear, slink away, and not let on to this sweet couple how totally incompetent I felt.

Betsy continued, "I think you're out here for a purpose, and if you quit, you will never know what it feels like to succeed."

Was she a mind reader? She was like a mother and a fairy godmother all wrapped in one. There was no doubt in my mind that neither she nor Cal would judge me or think me a failure.

"Yesterday was so hard. It began so good, so full of hope. Then the first stop I made to refuel, the clerk made me feel useless and unimportant. Like I wasn't worthy. I guess that set the tone for the rest of my trip."

Cal touched my arm. "And when I came over and stuck my nose into your business, you just deflated. I saw it right before my eyes. Like I had poked a pin in your balloon."

I pulled myself up straight. "I'm so sorry. It's just with the clerk and the rain, I got lost on a detour and went miles and miles out of my way. It reminded me of the hopelessness I felt when my husband was dying and there was nothing I could do. I swore that when I found the highway, I was headed home."

"Tell you what," Cal said. "How about we go over to your RV, and you can walk through the setup steps while I watch over your shoulder. That way if you have any questions, I'll be right there, but you do it all on your own, so you know what to do. Stay tomorrow, and if you still want to head home, we'll help you pack."

"But—"

"No buts," Betsy chimed in. "You owe it to yourself to see this through. Ain't none of us getting any younger. You deserve to finish this journey you started. There's nothing back home that's more important than fueling your soul, and you found just the place to begin that process. Right Cal?"

He squeezed her hand. "That's right, honey bunch."

"How are you so wise?" I asked.

She winked. "I've been there, hon. I don't know what your story is, but I know you're carrying a burden. Mine was five years ago. That's when Cal and I got together."

The shock must have shown on my face.

"That's right. We reconnected at a class reunion back home. You see, we were high school sweethearts and, well, one thing led to another, and we each married different partners. Mine was a tumultuous marriage. When we divorced, I swore off men and became bitter. A bitter de-vor-see, as my husband says."

Cal smiled sheepishly. "I was a widower who decided I could solve my problems with whiskey. Let me tell you, that doesn't solve anything."

"But a friend talked me into going to our class reunion. The last thing I wanted to do was sit around listening to a bunch of old people talking about their aches and pains," Betsy said. "But I went not expecting much. That's where I met back up with Cal. And time had not been good to him. But I felt a little flutter."

Cal laughed. "I was already about half-tanked. She walked right up to me and said, 'Calvin Bittner, you are a sloppy mess.' And I said, 'Yes ma'am, I am.' She ignored me the rest of the night. The next day, I called her and invited her to the VFW. Boy, did she let me have it."

"That's right," Betsy said. "I told him that I was a God-fearing woman who didn't put up with drunks. Then I hung up on him. About three months later, he called back and told me that I had saved his life. That he hadn't had a drink since our reunion."

"I must have charmed her, because we got married a year later."

"And the old coot still hasn't had a drink. So, Annie, whatever burden you're carrying, you need to see it through for your own sake and for those you love. Maybe staying here a few days might be what your soul needs to begin healing."

With neighbors like the Bittners, how could I refuse. I pushed my defeatist attitude aside and decided to stay. Maybe I would take a stab at the magazine article.

I waddled back to my RV with a belly full of biscuits and gravy and a foil-covered plate with sausage and biscuits for an easy breakfast tomorrow. True to his word, Cal came over and we walked through the entire setup, including leveling the RV and putting the slides out to make more room inside.

I spent the morning and the better part of the afternoon at my laptop working on my article. After breaking for a short walk around the campground, Calvin and Betsy invited me to a dinner of fried fish and potatoes along with a slice of Betsy's award-winning chocolate cream pie.

CHAPTER ELEVEN

I awoke before dawn and stepped outside with a cup of coffee. The sun had not risen, but a full moon shone over the campground, illuminating a thin layer of ground fog. The *clickity-clack* of a train echoed eerily in the distance. Next door a light in the Bittners' camper flicked off, and Cal emerged carrying a flashlight, fishing pole, and bucket. He waved when he saw me and ambled over.

"Morning, Ms. Annie. I'm heading down to the stream to drown some worms and watch the sunrise. You want to tag along?"

I couldn't remember ever watching the sunrise. Not on purpose anyway. Not that I slept in—I'd just never taken the time to step outside and wait for the sun to rise. Early mornings I could usually be found in my study hunched over my phone reading the news or playing a game while I drank my coffee. Only when I was sufficiently caffeinated would I step outside, and that was usually mid-morning, long after the sun had made an appearance.

Cal only carried one pole.

"What about Betsy? Is she sleeping in?"

"Heavens no. She's at the recreation center with the other

hens doing chair yogi. If you'd rather, you could join them and twist yourself into a pretzel."

I chuckled at his pronunciation of *yoga*. "Yeah, I probably should, but the morning is too nice to stay inside. Watching the sunrise sounds nice."

"If you don't mind jibber-jawing with an old man, grab Betsy's pole and let's go." Calvin nodded to a second pole leaning against their camper. "Got to hurry. We want to beat the sun. It's magical when it pops up over the hills. Nature is just now waking. We might get lucky and catch the mama and her fawn that come down every morning for a drink. Grab those two camp chairs while you're at it. We might as well be comfortable."

It wasn't like I had a full agenda today, and I had gotten so much done on my article yesterday that I felt like another day here would do me good. "Why not?" I set down my coffee, grabbed the pole and stools, and set off to find the sun.

"Didn't you catch a ton of fish yesterday?" I asked as we wandered down the gravel lane following the scant light of Cal's flashlight.

"Sure enough. Had so many that Betsy froze what she didn't cook last night. It's not about the fishing, missy. It's about communing with nature." Cal chuckled. "Most of the time I throw the little fellers back in and give them the chance to see another day."

His gentle nature amazed me. At the side of the stream, he unfolded the stools, pulled a small container from inside the bucket, and held it out. "You want to bait your hook?"

I scrunched my nose. "Worms?"

"Hand me that pole, young lady. My Betsy is squeam—" He stopped talking and placed a finger to his lips. "Shh. Look, the sun is starting to rise." He sank onto the stool and motioned for me to sit.

As we waited, purple and red hues stretched from the horizon, painting the eastern sky as the sun inched over the distant hills. Purple turned into lavender, and red turned into rose as the sun made its ascent. My breath caught as golden streaks of sunlight reached upward. Tears built behind my eyes when I realized that Michael and I had never watched the sunrise, and we never would. But here I was enjoying one now with someone I barely knew.

I felt a lightness in my heart that I hadn't felt in a long, long time. Maybe this trip would do me good. If one sunrise could inspire me, I could only imagine how seeing the sunrise morning after morning would affect me. Throw in a few sunsets to boot, and who knew what I could do.

Cal leaned in and whispered, "You're having a moment, aren't you?"

Words would not come, but I nodded and let the tears fall.

Cal sat quietly by my side. How he knew what I needed, I didn't know, but instead of trying to console me, he bowed his head and waited for me to pull myself together.

I scrubbed my eyes with the heels of my hands and took a deep breath that cleansed my soul. "Whew."

"You okay?" he asked in a gentle tone.

"I am." And I thought I was, or at least I was on the right path. Thanks to the Bittners and whatever magic potion they possessed, I felt ready to continue my trip.

"Take a look over there," he said.

I followed his gaze to a small clearing on the other side of the stream.

"There they are."

A mama doe stood tentatively at the water's edge, scanning the area. "Where's the baby?" I whispered back.

"Hang on. He's hiding in the brush. Mama's checking her

surroundings. She'll call the little feller when she thinks it's safe."

Less than a minute later, a small spotted fawn burst out of the brush, jumping and kicking its heels. Mama drank from the stream while her fawn scampered around the clearing. In a nearby tree, a chattering noise caused Mama to jerk to attention.

"What was that?" I asked.

Cal pointed to a branch extending over the water. A fat squirrel sat at the tip of the branch, twitching its tail and chattering.

The deer jerked its head again and bounded off into the brush, the fawn close on her heels.

"That was amazing. I've never seen a deer that close."

Cal smiled and placed a worm on my hook. "Toss that line in the water and let's catch some fish."

We sat there watching the bobbers rise and fall. When mine went under and stayed under, and I felt a gentle tug on my line, I held out my pole to Cal. "I think I have one."

Cal ignored it. "You do indeed. Reel it in. You got this."

I knew he meant more than the fish on the end of my line. "Come to mama, little fishy." I furiously twisted the handle on the reel.

Cal laid a hand on my shoulder. "Slowly. Give and take." He demonstrated with his own pole.

I watched his rhythm as he worked the reel and followed with my own. When my fish broke the surface, I squealed. "He's a big one. My very first fish, and he's a whopper."

Cal grabbed a small net from inside the bucket. "Pull him in. I'll catch him in the net."

I dropped the fish into the net, and Cal dipped the bucket into the stream and filled it with water. He removed my fish from the hook and dropped it in the bucket.

"Weren't we going to throw him back in?"

"Not your very first fish, Ms. Annie. You'll want this guy for dinner, won't you?"

"No. He needs his freedom more than I need a meal. Let's give him another day. He probably has a fish family waiting for him."

"Good call." Cal handed me the bucket. "You want to do the honors?"

I took the bucket and gently tipped it into the water. "Have a good life, little guy, and steer clear of worms."

We threw our lines back in and continued fishing for another hour with nary a bite. When the sun had fully risen, Cal looked at his watch. "You had enough? Betsy will be home by now, and she'll have breakfast waiting."

We gathered our things and headed back to the campsite. When we arrived, I set my pole against the Bittners' camper where I'd found it.

Betsy stood in the door wiping her hands on an apron tied around her waist. "Y'all have a sit at the picnic table, and I'll bring breakfast out."

I started to protest, but Betsy quickly replied, "I won't take no for an answer. We have enough food for an army. Besides, you put up with Calvin. I owe you one. Sit yourself down and let me pamper you."

Several hours later and after great conversation, I left the Bittners and walked back to my RV. After I showered and changed, I took my laptop and phone outside. A text pinged my phone.

KAITLYN: HOPE YOUR TRIP IS GOING WELL.

ME: IT IS. THANKS!

KAITLYN: HAVE YOU TALKED TO UNCLE TIM?

ME: I LET HIM KNOW I WAS HERE. HEADING TO NASHVILLE IN THE MORNING. TALK TO YOU TOMORROW. LOVE YOU.

I'd no sooner set the phone down and opened my laptop than the phone rang. Before I even looked at the display, I knew it was Tim.

"Hey," I said.

"Hey yourself. How's it going?"

"Had a rough start, but I think I'm getting the hang of it. Setting up the RV in the comfort of my driveway versus actually doing it in a campground is a bit challenging. But with the help of a neighbor, I'm all set. Though I have to reverse the process tomorrow when I head to Nashville."

"Pretty soon you'll be an old pro," Tim said.

"Not likely. I just want to make it through this trip. I did start my project, and it's feeling good to stretch my brain muscles."

"Good to hear. I won't keep you. Just wanted to make sure you were doing okay."

"Thanks." I said goodbye and disconnected. The peace and contentment I'd felt today surrounded me like a comforting blanket.

CHAPTER TWELVE

I rose before dawn, hoping to catch Cal. The light in their camper was off, and their car was gone. Worry settled in. Where would they have gone before daylight? My thoughts all went to the dark side, of course. Both Cal and Betsy were well into their eighties, and any number of things could explain their sudden departure, but medical jumped to the top of my list. I startled when a golf cart putted up the road and stopped in front of my RV.

I recognized the manager of the campground, Lettie. "Sorry to disturb you this early, but Cal said you'd be awake."

"Are they okay? I worried when I didn't see their car."

"Yes, they're fine. Betsy's granddaughter called, and her babysitter isn't going to be able to get the kids off to school. Cal drove her into town to sit with the kids until school starts. He said to tell you they'd be back around nine. If you want to catch the mama and her baby, he said you'd best get yourself down to the stream."

I relaxed and took a deep breath. "Thank goodness they're okay."

"They're fine."

"I thought they were from Tennessee."

She laughed. "They are. Their kids are scattered all over the country. He has two, and Betsy has four. They travel around visiting their children and grandchildren and stay two months each place. Betsy's daughter lives here in Settler's Grove."

"They don't ever go home?"

Lettie chuckled. "They sold their homes when they got married and bought the RV. I better get back. Yoga will be starting soon, and I need to be there. You're welcome to join us."

I could do yoga at home. For that matter, I could watch the sunrise from my patio—which I now planned to do on a regular basis—but the chances of seeing a doe and her fawn in my backyard were slim. "I appreciate the offer, but I think I'll take a walk down to the stream and watch the sunrise."

After she drove away, I noticed Cal had left a pole and a container of worms on my picnic table. I wondered if I had the guts to bait my own hook. I'd had the guts to embark on this trip by myself. How could putting a worm on a hook be more difficult.

My trip to the stream made me wish for another morning here, but I had reservations waiting in Nashville. I returned to the RV hoping I'd see the Bittners before I had to leave. Cal would be proud that I'd not only baited the hook, but I'd caught another fish, which I promptly released.

When I had the RV ready to go and was settled in the driver's seat, the Bittners drove up.

"Hey, Annie," Cal said when I climbed out the door. "We were hoping to see you before you left."

Betsy ambled over and hugged me. "You take care of yourself."

"And drive safely," Cal added. "You got everything buckled up good?"

I nodded. "I followed the list and double-checked everything."

"How about inside? Don't leave anything out that can get loose," Betsy said.

"I'm good. Did a thorough walk through, and everything is put away and locked down."

Betsy gave me an index card with their email address and made me promise to keep in touch. Calvin slipped me another one with his cell number and told me to call if I had any trouble along the way.

I sucked in a deep breath as they took turns hugging me. Emotions churned through me as I said goodbye to this couple who had helped me get back into the RV and not turn tail and race home. Instead, they had given me the courage to continue this journey I so needed to complete. I didn't know what lay ahead of me, but I knew that encouragement was only an email or phone call away.

"You got this, girl." Cal gave me a thumbs-up.

My eyes watered as I pulled onto the main road and headed toward Nashville.

I had reserved two nights at a small campground outside of Nashville. I'd also scored a ticket to a concert at Ryman Auditorium for tonight and another for the Grand Ole Opry the following night. Nashville was one of the first places Michael and I had visited after we got married. We'd been so excited that we hadn't thought to buy tickets in advance. We didn't get to go to concerts at either venue, so we made do visiting some of the local dives where unknown artists tried to get the ear of a talent agent or manager. Those kinds of places were more in line with our budget.

Somewhere near Chattanooga, I missed a turn and drove twenty miles out of the way before I realized I wasn't on the right highway. I hadn't programmed Nashville into the GPS because it was a straight shot, or so I'd thought. Lesson learned. At least this time, I felt more comfortable driving Monroe and it wasn't raining. I also knew where I had made my mistake and could easily fix it.

Before turning around, I pulled into Big Chuck's Café for a glass of sweet tea and a leg stretch. An attractive young woman with long black hair occupied a booth near the door. She looked up when I walked in and quickly averted her eyes, but not before I saw her tear-stained cheeks. The rest of the place was vacant except for a burly guy standing behind the counter paging through a newspaper. An unlit cigarette dangled from his lips. He wore a white sleeveless T-shirt. Big Chuck, I presumed. I slid into a booth and pulled a cracked, plastic menu from between the wall and napkin holder.

"Janine, you got a customer!" the burly guy hollered over his shoulder. "Get out here on the double."

"Hold your shorts on, Chuck," a raspy voice answered.

I checked the menu, trying desperately not to look at my surroundings. Big Chuck's Café was the textbook example of depressing. The beadboard walls were painted seafoam green. Large, faded posters of Big Chuck's menu items hung in cheap aluminum frames in each window along the front of the restaurant. Worn linoleum marked the paths Janine took each day from the kitchen to each table.

The waitress appeared and set a cracked brown tumbler filled with water in front of me. "Know what you want?" She wore a limp white uniform with her name tag pinned in the center of a red lace hanky near her left shoulder. A black apron clung to her skinny hips like a gunslinger's belt.

"Sweet tea."

"Anything else?"

I glanced at the water she'd delivered. "No. Can I have the tea in a to-go cup, please?"

She pulled a pencil from somewhere in her froth of curly

magenta hair. "That'll cost you ten cents extra. We don't give those cups away."

"That's fine."

She turned and stopped abruptly. "Where'd that girl go?"

Big Chuck folded his newspaper. "She was here a minute ago."

"That little delinquent left without paying her ticket." Janine ran out the front door screaming profanities. Outside, she stopped, shaded her eyes, and scanned all directions.

Except for Monroe and a rusty Geo Tracker, the parking lot was vacant. Janine stalked back inside and threw her order pad on the counter in front of Big Chuck. "I ain't paying her ticket, Chuck. You were standing here when she took off in broad daylight. You ought to call the damn sheriff. She can't have got far."

"Your table, your responsibility." Chuck rolled the cigarette around his mouth like he really wanted to light up. "You know the rules."

Janine snatched a foam cup from a round tube hanging on the wall behind the counter and filled it with ice and tea. "You lousy ass. You were standing here same as me. I'm getting sick and tired of paying off the tickets of your deadbeat customers."

Chuck snorted. "Then watch your damn tables. This is the fourth one you let get away this week. I can't be cooking and watching over your shoulder every minute of the day." He tucked the newspaper under his arm and disappeared into the men's room.

"You weren't cooking, you idiot. You are standing right there." Janine shot him a killer look. If she'd had a knife in her hand, it wouldn't have surprised me if she plunged it in between his shoulder blades.

When Janine finally brought my tea to the table, she set it down with enough force that the lid popped off. "That'll be two dollars and forty-nine cents—now. I ain't having you run out on me too."

"How much did she owe?" I asked, feeling sorry for the girl. I didn't know if Janine or Chuck would call the sheriff, but one thing I did know. The girl was in trouble, and not having enough money to cover her meal was only part of it. Having to deal with law enforcement would only cause her more problems. "I'll cover it."

Janine paused and eyed me. "Let's see. She had a loaded cheeseburger, onion rings, a piece of cherry pie, and a chocolate malt. With tax and a tip, it came to fifteen dollars and twenty-five cents."

I took a twenty from my wallet and handed it to her. "This should cover it."

She stuffed the money in her pocket without saying thanks.

CHAPTER THIRTEEN

After consulting my GPS and finding my error, I pulled Monroe onto the highway and headed back to Chattanooga. I half expected to see the young woman along the highway. Even though it was a stupid idea, one that I would have scolded Kaitlyn for, I decided to ignore the consequences of picking up a hitchhiker. But I didn't get the chance. She'd either gone the opposite direction or had already been picked up by another passerby. I crossed my fingers and said a prayer for her. The thought of her being on the road by herself made my heart hurt.

Chattanooga came and went, though not quickly enough. Monroe struggled through the hills and curves, and I breathed a sigh of relief when the road finally leveled and straightened. I arrived at my campground, ran through my checklist to get Monroe ready, and still had time before the concert to stroll around the campground. It wasn't as pretty or serene as my previous location. Gravel roads wound through the facility, and each site had a small tree. It would take years before the saplings provided shade or privacy.

I did find a small lake and thought that might be a perfect spot to watch the sun come up. Campers of all sizes and shapes filled the sites, and the license plates attested to the distances people would drive for vacation. I spotted several from Kentucky, Missouri, Ontario, California, and Delaware.

None of the campers looked like they'd set up residence like the Bittners had. A few had awnings open with lawn chairs scattered in the tiny yards, but there were no flowers, lawn decorations, or tiny twinkly lights, and there were children—lots of children. In the road in front of Monroe, an impromptu kickball game had commenced, and children of all ages vied for positions.

I found a bench and settled in to watch the game. Would Kaitlyn and Kyle have fit in as easily as these children did? Michael and I had stopped camping by the time they came along. I'd organized all their activities to an *n*th degree so their schedules didn't conflict with Michael's, so he could attend. Though he was rarely home for dinner, I'd made sure to put a meal on the table precisely at six each evening. Michael had never appreciated the difficulty of raising the children around his schedule. And I wondered why he'd softened in the months before his death. Did he have other regrets in life besides missing vacations?

He never missed little league games with Kyle or dance recitals with Kaitlyn. But most years he missed our anniversary. He'd come home from work for the occasion, but like any other night, he'd leave his briefcase in his study and stroll to the kitchen for a beer. If I was there, he might drop a kiss on my neck and return to his study where I would have left an anniversary card and a small gift—usually something I'd mulled over for weeks and then spent a small fortune on.

My cell phone rang, snapping me back to the present. Tim's number appeared on the display.

"Everything okay?" I asked, answering the phone.

"Yes. Just checking in. Figured you should be in Nashville by now."

"I am. Took a detour this morning on the way but nothing bad. Got to see more of Tennessee than I had anticipated."

He laughed. "Bet you missed the exit. I've done that myself. That exit sneaks up on you. Are you having any trouble with the motor home?"

"Other than sucking down the fuel, he seems to be doing pretty good." I ducked when a ball flew my way.

"Sorry!" a towhead boy yelled and zipped past me to retrieve it. The little girl who had kicked it scuffed the ground with her toe in disgust.

"He?" Tim asked. "Who's doing good?"

"The RV. I started calling it Monroe." Now, why had I told him that? He'd think I was losing my mind.

"Ah, good plan. I just wanted to check in and see how you're doing."

"Is that all?" I asked.

"Y—" Tim hesitated.

"Well?"

"No," he said. "Look, I know I can't make up for the time we lost after Michael's death. There will never be enough sorrys. But dammit, Annie, you and I have a history. I don't want to lose that over a stupid mistake. Can we rewind our friendship? Go back to where we were before Michael died?"

"Tim, look—"

"No, wait, let me finish before you answer that question. I know I let you down when you needed a friend the most. I can't make that up to you. I should have been there to help you through your grief. Eww, did that sound creepy? I didn't mean it to sound creepy."

"No, it didn't sound creepy. But Tim, there's a lot I need to tell you. A lot you don't know about Michael and me. At least, I don't think you know." Was now the time to start this dialogue? Maybe on the phone rather than in person. I didn't know if I could look Tim in the eyes and tell him about the facade Michael and I had been living. I didn't know if we could still be friends after he learned of our deception. And mostly I didn't want his view of Michael to change. But I didn't know if I could resurrect our friendship without coming clean. Michael had always been my buffer, my partner in crime, in that facade. Now it was just me. I was far from perfect, and honestly, I was tired of living a lie. If I was going to make a clean break from my past and move forward, I had to tell Tim. If it damaged our friendship, then so be it.

"What's to know about the perfect couple? You guys were like a made-for-television family sitcom. I felt so fortunate to be an unofficial member. When Kaitlyn and Kyle started calling me Uncle Tim—" He stopped abruptly, his voice growing husky.

No time like the present. "Tim, stop. Michael and I were not perfect. We were not the perfect family. On the outside, maybe. But on the inside, we were . . ." I could not do this. It was like ripping away years of scabs to reveal horrendous oozing sores. I bit my cheek. "Look, can we do this another time?"

"What? Sure," Tim said. "Annie, I don't want to put you on the spot. If you're still angry with me, I get it. I just want you to do something you love. I know it can't be easy for you."

"It's not that. We can move past the anger. We are moving past it. I was more hurt than anything, and it just came out as anger. But . . . I can't do this now." I disconnected and took several deep breaths to settle all the feelings churning inside me. If Tim could be patient, I could do this, but I needed to take small baby steps.

CHAPTER FOURTEEN

The concert and Ryman Auditorium exceeded my expectations. It was past midnight by the time I returned to the campground and fell into bed—still in jeans and my newly purchased cowboy boots. Around three in the morning, the boots started pinching my toes, and I had to ditch them.

I lolled in bed until nine. Sad that I'd missed the sunrise, I donned my walking shoes for a stroll around the camp and replayed last night's conversation with Tim. Could I really confide in him? We'd both been scarred after losing Michael. Michael was my husband, but he'd been Tim's best friend all their lives. Would he resent me if my admission put Michael in a bad light? Tim and I were once so close, he knew my thoughts before I voiced them. Had he not seen how unhappy I was? How dysfunctional Michael and I were? Or had he chosen to ignore it? That seemed far more likely. Always the peacemaker, he would close his eyes to a problem rather than face it head-on. Much like he had after Michael and I had connected the night of the Barrister's Ball.

When Tim returned to campus after visiting his ailing mother, Michael declared that he and I were an item. Tim humbly stepped aside, satisfied to be our third wheel. Never once had he stood up to Michael. Never once had he asked me why. Never once had he fought for me. And that one night was all it took for me to get pregnant. When that happened, Michael and I were quickly married, and thus our life together began.

I got so lost in my thoughts, I didn't notice a giant pothole in the road and went down hard. The jolt reverberated throughout my body, and I lay there for a moment trying to get my wits together.

"Hey, are you okay?" a man's voice asked.

I pushed onto my hands and knees and squealed with pain. "My knee."

He reached for my elbow. "Let me help."

"Give me a minute to catch my breath." I stared into the coffee-brown eyes of a man about my age who wore lime green and black shorts with a matching sleeveless tee.

"Let me look at that knee. I'll be right back." He jogged over to a mountain bike that leaned against a nearby tree and retrieved a small pouch and a bottle of water.

"I'm okay, really." Embarrassment had set in, and at this point, I just wanted to be left alone to wallow in my stupidness.

"This will only take a minute." He pulled a cloth from the pouch and wet it. "Let's get that cleaned and have a look, shall we?"

"I'm fine. You don't need to go to the trouble. I just need a minute."

I sat there, uncomfortable with the attention and worried I couldn't stand on my own without further embarrassing myself. My palms stung, my left knee throbbed, and the little finger on my right hand was swelling.

The man grinned. "It's no trouble." He bent down.

I raised my hands in front of me. "I said I'm fine. Can you just leave me alone?"

He stood. "Can I at least help you to your feet? I don't feel right leaving and not knowing if you can walk or not."

"Fine." I reached for his outstretched hand and bit my tongue to keep from yelping when I stood. "Thanks. I can take it from here." I took a step to test my knee and wobbled when my knee started to buckle.

"Take my arm and lean on me."

"I'm fine. I just need to stand here a minute and get my wits." *Leave me alone.* I didn't want to appear ungrateful, but all the attention only highlighted my stupidity.

"Are you staying at the campground?"

I nodded.

"You certainly have an independent streak. Do you want me to stop by your RV and let your husband know?"

I wasn't about to admit to being alone. He could be a serial killer.

"No, I'm fine." I hobbled a few steps to show him I didn't need his help. "I'll take it slow. I promise. Now please, go on back to your ride and let me have some dignity."

"Okay, but if you need anything at all, let me know. I'm Keith. My RV is the blue section, number fourteen. I'm in the second space from the trailhead."

Great! His RV was parked next to mine. "Annie," I said, purposely omitting my last name.

"Okay, if you're sure, Annie."

"One hundred percent."

"Keep the water." He handed me the bottle and returned the supplies to his bike.

Before he pedaled off, he looked over his shoulder. "You sure?"

I waved him on and waited until he was out of sight to try another step. Pain shot up my leg. I bent to brush the gravel away from my knee. The gash didn't look terribly deep, more like a severe rash. I tested another step and another, limping to keep as much weight off my leg as possible. I grimaced and clenched my jaw with each step. At this rate, it would take me forever to get back to the RV.

I hobbled over to a stone outcropping and sat down. It felt good to have the weight off my leg. If I sat for a few minutes and rested my knee, maybe I could take a few steps at a time and rest along the way. I poured water over my wound, washing away the blood and the rest of the gravel. It stung like crazy. After inspecting it, I reluctantly pulled my shirt off, thankful I had a sports bra underneath, and carefully wrapped it tightly around my knee. I pulled the sleeves together under my kneecap and tied them.

With the additional support, I took a deep breath and stood, testing the weight on my leg. Not so bad. I took a few more steps, calculating how far I was from my RV.

"You idiot," I mumbled. "Why is it so hard to accept help?" If I had been willing to accept the biker guy's help, I'd be back at the RV now with my leg propped up on a pillow, and I'd be sipping on a glass of iced tea. *Yeah, you could be tied up in the trunk of his car headed to some rundown shack in the middle of nowhere too.* I took three more steps. At this rate, I'd be here until well after dark. That rundown shack was starting to sound good. So much for my concert tonight. I'd be listening to crickets and bugs instead.

The *putt putt* of a golf cart caught my attention. Thank heavens there was someone else on the trail. I quickly untied my shirt and slipped it on. God forbid, I get caught in the woods in nothing but a sports bra and shorts. I was in decent shape, but the world was not ready to see my midriff.

When I saw the golf cart coming from the direction of the campground, I waved, hoping they'd stop and give me a lift to my RV.

A grinning Keith pulled up next to me and stopped. "You're making pretty good time."

I groaned. "Shut up and give me a ride."

He looked over his shoulder and shrugged. "I guess I

could stop on my way back and get you if you haven't made it back."

"Are you kidding?"

"No ma'am. I am not a kidder."

"Okay, I'm sorry. Now can I have a ride?"

He hopped off the cart and hurried around to the passenger side. "Of course. I just wanted to hear you say you were sorry."

"Thanks," I said through gritted teeth.

He helped me get situated in the cart, handed me an ice pack, and made sure I was comfortable before taking off.

When he pulled up in front of my RV, I said, "How did you know which one was mine?"

"Easy. I went to the office and asked them where the stubborn independent lady was staying, so I could tell her husband where she was. Imagine my surprise when I learned you were my neighbor with no husband to come to your rescue. So, I did what any good neighbor does. I borrowed the cart, put on my white hat, and mounted my trusty steed to come to your aid."

"Very funny. You obviously watch too many westerns. But thank you again." I eased off the cart tentatively. Twice in one week, a stranger had helped me. I was used to that at home with neighbors I had lived by for ages. But for people who didn't know me to help was something new. I had to wonder if this was some sort of campground etiquette.

"Not so fast, fair damsel," Keith said. "Stay right there. I'm going to bring my truck around and haul your stubborn butt off to urgent care."

"What? No, I don't need to go to urgent care."

"Yeah, and you don't need help getting off the trail either. Either you let me take you to get that knee x-rayed, or I'll haul you back down the trail and you can hoof it back on your own. Now sit down until I get back."

"Did anyone ever tell you that you're bossy?"

"I seem to recall my ex-wife saying that a time or two. That's why she's my ex."

It was well into the afternoon by the time we returned from urgent care. The diagnosis was scrapes and contusions. Nothing broken. Keith helped me into the RV and got me situated on the couch.

"What can I get for you before I leave?" he asked.

"Nothing. I'm good." I reached for my laptop, which was just out of reach.

He raced over and handed it to me. "Don't start this again. I happen to know you haven't had lunch. What do you have to make a sandwich?" He opened the fridge and inspected the contents.

Before I could answer, he'd pulled out packages of ham and cheese. "Are you a mustard or mayo person?"

I sighed. "Mayo."

He quickly assembled two sandwiches, placing them on paper plates with a mound of chips on each plate.

"There's iced tea in there too," I said.

"That's more like it." He set the plate on top of my laptop and filled two tumblers with tea.

"Thank you."

He went to the door and turned. "I'll bring your glass back this evening when I bring you dinner."

"Oh, sit down," I said but quickly added, "and you don't have to bring me dinner."

He shrugged. "We'll see."

"Can I ask you a question?" I pulled the top slice of bread off my sandwich and inspected it.

"Did I poison your lunch?"

"What?"

"The way you're checking that sandwich makes me think

you're afraid I dosed it with some dastardly drug so I could have my way with you." He laughed. "Want to trade?"

"No, smart-ass. I was looking to see if you put the mayo on the ham or cheese side."

"I believe in equal opportunity. It's on both sides." He took a big bite of his sandwich and made moaning noises as he ate.

A sharp rap on the door startled me awake. Before I could get my wits about me, the door opened, and Keith strolled in carrying a pizza box and two longnecks.

"Dinner has arrived." He set the box down and pulled paper plates from the cabinet.

I pushed the throw off me and sat up. "What? What time is it?"

"A little after six. You fell asleep after we ate, so I tossed that cover on you and left."

"Crap! I'm going to be late." I stood up too quickly and grimaced when pain shot up my leg.

He laughed. "Very funny. You're not going anywhere, remember? Doctor's orders. He said you need to rest that leg and keep it elevated and wrapped." He retrieved the melted ice pack that had slid to the floor. "Lie back down while I get more ice."

"I can't. I have tickets for the Grand Ole Opry tonight."

"That's disappointing, but even if you could manage it by the time you got home, that knee would be three times bigger than it already is. The Grand Ole Opry has been around almost a hundred years. It'll be here the next time you're in town."

"But—"

He shook his head. "If you want a concert, and feel up to it, I'll take you up to the pavilion after we eat. There's a nightly jam session. The finest musicians this campground has to offer. And if you're extra good and clean your plate, I might even sing a tune or two."

"Seriously? You sing?"

"Not good, mind you, but if you drink enough, you might think I sound a bit like George Strait."

"Count me in. Are all campgrounds like this?"

"Like what?" He opened the beers and handed one to me.

"Friendly. The last campground, my neighbors were friendlier than folks in my hometown that I've known forever. And here, well, a concert every night. Do these people even know one another?"

"Some do. Others just wander over and join in. It's a community of like-minded people. And it is Nashville, so music is definitely involved."

I had one more thing to write about and something to be on the lookout for at my next stop. My first attempt—which still needed work—would be an ongoing theme of my project and dealt with facing the unknown. And the unknown, of course, meant meeting strangers and learning not to let fear stand in the way. Ugh, was I up for the task? Was I trying to take too many steps forward? Nagging doubts filled my brain as I wrestled with the positive aspects of this trip. I needed to focus on those. And right now, I had pizza. That and the fact that, for the second time, I would be missing the Grand Ole Opry.

Keith filled two plates with pizza slices and handed one to me, then dropped into the driver's captain's chair. When he swiveled around, his eyes landed on Michael's urn. "Is that what I think it is?"

I nodded and finished chewing. "My late husband."

He rose quickly, almost kicking over the beer he'd set at his feet. "Oh crap. I'm sorry. I'll leave you alone."

"You're fine. Sit down."

He glanced at the urn warily. "Umm, are you sure?"

"Yes." I explained about Michael's death without going into a lot of detail and that I'd decided use the trip to find a place to spread his ashes.

He settled into the chair but couldn't keep his eyes from wandering to the urn.

I held up the throw I'd been using. "You can cover it if it will make you more comfortable."

He took a chug of his beer and swallowed. "No, it's okay. Really."

We ate our pizza in silence. When we'd finished, he gathered our plates and empty bottles and disposed of them.

"Well, I guess I'll let you get some rest."

"Wait," I said. "You promised me a concert complete with a fake George Strait."

CHAPTER FIFTEEN

A little before sunrise, I stepped outside with my coffee to enjoy the morning before beginning my trek to Illinois. My knee still throbbed from my fall, so I passed on my walk to the lake.

Keith was at his picnic table with a coffee cup. "You're up early."

"Wanted to see the sunrise in Tennessee. Never realized how much I took them for granted."

"Have you changed your mind about leaving?" he asked.

I'd made the announcement last night when we were at the jam session. He had tried to talk me into staying a few days extra, but I had declined since I'd already made reservations in southern Illinois.

"Afraid not. As soon as the sun rises, and I get everything ready, I'm going to head out." I raised my cup and drained it.

"Can I at least help you get the RV ready? That knee is going to give you a fit."

My first instinct was to say no, but this was a journey to a new me. I had to keep getting my feet wet. "That would be appreciated."

About that time, the sun broke over the horizon and filled

the sky with a glorious light. I smiled and wondered what the day would hold for me.

***

When I reviewed my route yesterday, I noticed a ferry crossing at the Ohio River and opted for the long way around. I'd rather cross a body of water on a sturdy bridge than take my chances with Monroe on a ferry. I didn't even know if Monroe would fit on a ferry, and I didn't want to find out. Something about watching swirling water mere feet from my windshield did not sit well with me.

At Metropolis, Illinois, I stopped to catch a glimpse of Superman—the statue. Michael and I had visited here on our first camping trip. I decided to step out of my comfort zone and ask a couple to take a photo of me with the Man of Steel. I'd text the photos to Kaitlyn. She'd get a kick out of it.

Before I turned off onto the back road that led to Cave-in-Rock, I stopped for lunch. Even though Tim had stocked Monroe's kitchen, nothing appealed to me. A greasy spoon hamburger sounded like a real treat—but something a tad classier than Big Chuck's Café. I turned in to the next diner and parked Monroe. Kaitlyn called to laugh about the photo I'd sent. I grabbed my purse and headed into the restaurant while I told her all about Superman. When I walked inside, the same girl I'd seen at Big Chuck's Café sat in the booth closest to the door, scanning the menu. I did a double take. What were the chances?

"Katie," I said. "I have to go. Talk to you tonight when I get settled." I disconnected and dropped into the booth opposite the young woman. "You owe me fifteen dollars and twenty-five cents."

She looked over the menu she held. "What?"

I returned my phone to my purse. "Day before yesterday

at Big Chuck's Café, you skipped out on your bill, and I paid it."

She laughed and laid the menu down. "Then you got scammed. Or else those were the most expensive fries on the planet."

A weary-looking waitress stopped by our table. "You two know what you want?"

I shook my head. "Give us a minute."

She shrugged and called over her shoulder as she retreated, "My name's Candy. Let me know when you're ready."

"All you had was an order of fries?" I asked, thinking that Janine had compensated for a few of her walk-offs at my expense.

"Yes ma'am." She laughed. "Fries and a glass of water."

I squared my shoulders, pushing back my embarrassment at being taken so easily. "You still left without paying your ticket. That's stealing."

She ducked her head, her cheeks stained with color. "It was wrong, I know."

Three truckers filed through the door and took seats at the counter. Candy animatedly filled coffee cups and took orders. Apparently, waiting on women wore her out.

"Where are you headed?" I motioned to Candy that we were ready to order.

"Wherever the road leads me," the young woman said.

When Candy appeared, I ordered burgers, fries, and strawberry shakes for two. Candy committed our order to memory and headed for the kitchen.

"I can't afford that."

"Don't worry about it. It's on me. I'm Annie, by the way." I offered my hand, but she ignored me.

"I'm Savannah. Are you some kind of weirdo?"

"No, I saw that you were upset the other day. I wanted to

help, but you disappeared before I could talk to you. Imagine my surprise to see you here."

She shifted in the booth and pulled a backpack from under the table. "I got to get going."

"You have a busy schedule to keep?" I reached across the table and touched her hand. "We got burgers coming. You can at least stay for that, can't you? That's the least you can do to repay me."

She jerked back, glanced around the room, and then looked back at me. "Why are you doing this? What do you want?"

"Someone has to keep you from skipping out and making that poor waitress buy your lunch."

She sneered. "They just write it off."

I shook my head. "More often than not, the server is responsible for the difference."

Her eyes widened. "Really?"

"Yes."

Our burgers arrived, and Savannah tucked into hers without prompting. She didn't stop until she'd polished off half the burger and a dozen fries. "That why you paid for my lunch at the other place?"

"Yes. Only it seems you weren't the only dishonest person in that establishment. Were you going to leave without paying here too?"

Savannah sighed. "You're really nosy."

"I've been told that a time or two," I admitted. Kaitlyn and Kyle used to tell me I was nosy on a regular basis. I chose to believe it was the mark of a concerned parent. Along with setting curfews when they went out, I also wanted to know who they would be with and where they were going—all things that irritated them to no end when they were growing up.

"I was going to order a glass of water, if you have to know." She squirted a puddle of ketchup on her plate and pulled a fry through it.

I finished off my burger and pushed my plate aside. "You really expect me to believe that?"

"You can believe what you want. It's a free world. You going to eat those fries?" She pointed to the stragglers I'd left.

"Go ahead."

The truckers paid their bills and headed out the door to their rigs.

I slid out of the booth. "I'll be right back. Going to visit the restroom. If the waitress comes back, order me a Coke to-go. Order one for yourself, if you want."

When I returned, Savannah had disappeared. I hadn't counted on that. I'd assumed since she didn't need to ditch out on her ticket, she'd still be there when I returned. My Coke in the to-go cup sat on top of the bill. I flagged Candy down to pay for the meal. "Where'd the girl go?"

"Beats me. Hightailed it right after you went to the john. Told me to bring the Coke for you." She handed me the ticket. "Probably got a ride from one of them truckers. That's how she got here early this morning. Been sitting here ever since. After I saw you come in, I figured she'd been waiting for you. Guess not. Looks like she pulled one over on you."

I drove along the highway looking for Savannah in case she was still hitchhiking, but when I didn't find her, I headed to Cave-in-Rock State Park. Soon after I started down the black-top, the road narrowed. The straight lane gave way to curves and hills. Monroe hugged the road like a champ, but the fact that there were no shoulders scared me. I reduced my speed and focused on driving.

After one particularly bad curve, a noise coming from the bathroom caught my attention. I hadn't had any plumbing problems and hoped the bumpy road hadn't torn something apart. There was no place to pull over, and I kept going. If the sewage lines had broken, I'd take care of it when I got to the park. Though, I sure didn't look forward to the prospect of cleaning a mess.

I arrived at the park and checked in. Once I had Monroe situated, I headed to the bathroom to check on my plumbing problem. Just as I reached for the doorknob, a retching sound came from inside. I jerked open the door and found Savannah bent over the toilet.

I screamed and jumped back. She clung to the toilet, sweat rolling down her face.

"You scared me," I said.

She looked at me with pleading eyes. "I'm really sick."

I got a washcloth, dampened it, and dabbed her face. "This will help," I said for lack of something better. It reminded me of all the times I'd nursed my children through bouts of tummy issues. White soda and chicken noodle soup had always been my go-tos when my kids were sick. More recently it reminded me of Michael's final days. Nothing I had done eased his nausea.

She mumbled something about not feeling well again and promptly vomited.

I fumbled in my cosmetic bag for a hair band and pulled her hair into a ponytail to get it off her face. "Hold this cloth, and I'll get you something to calm your stomach."

I checked the first aid supplies Tim had put together. Finding nothing for an upset stomach, I rummaged in the fridge for a can of white soda. I poured a little into a glass and grabbed a package of crackers from the cabinet.

"Here," I said. "Take small sips of this and a few bites of the cracker. They should ease your stomach."

Savannah leaned her head against the wall and took a long drink.

"Slow down. Let it sit for a minute to see if it's going to stay down." I re-wet the cloth and wiped her forehead again. "If that works, you can try the crackers. Don't force yourself. Just take it easy."

She groaned and hunched over, holding her stomach.

I patted, then rubbed her back just like I had done with Michael those last months. Had his distance for all those years jaded me? Had my anger made me less responsive to his final needs? Had I given my all to make him comfortable? Could I have done something different? Could I have at least tried to clear the air with him?

"Thank you," Savannah muttered. "Can I try the crackers?"

I slipped one from the sleeve and handed it to her.

She took a tentative bite. "Shouldn't have eaten that stupid burger."

"I had the same thing, and I'm fine. How long has it been since you've eaten before the burger?"

She shrugged.

I slid to the floor outside the bathroom, keeping the door open. "How long have you been hitchhiking?"

"A couple of days?"

"I know you've been hitchhiking at least two days. How many before that?"

"Maybe a week," she said.

So many questions rattled around my brain, but now was not the time to bombard her. She looked so young and vulnerable sitting there. Possibly a runaway. Or escaping an abusive relationship. Didn't matter for now. My priority was getting her back on her feet and deciding what to do with her. There was no way I'd leave her on the side of the road to hitchhike again. I kept thinking about how kind the Bittners and Keith had been to me and how Keith had told me about the friendly atmosphere of campgrounds. The least I could do was extend that friendship to her. Once she was feeling better, I'd need more information before I decided my next move. If she was an underage runaway, I'd have to involve law enforcement, unless she called her parents first. I'd at least give her that opportunity.

Slowly, the color returned to her face. "I think it's working. I don't feel as woozy."

"Can you stand?" I wanted to get her to the couch to lie down, but not if there was a chance she'd get sick again.

She nodded and got to her feet, using the toilet to steady herself. "Whoa! Everything's swirling. Let me stand here for a minute."

"Stay here until I get back." I headed to the bedroom and pulled a sheet, pillow, and blanket from the closet and rushed to make up the couch. Afterward, I took a plastic waste can from under the sink, lined it with a grocery bag, and placed it beside the couch.

"Come and lie down. Let's not rush things." I led her to the couch and propped the pillow under her head. I pointed to the waste can. "If you feel like you're going to be sick, use this."

She smiled wanly. "Thanks."

"Don't thank me. You've got some explaining to do, but not until I know you're not going to toss your cookies."

CHAPTER SIXTEEN

Savannah fell asleep almost as soon as she hit the pillow. I let her sleep and took my laptop outside to a nearby picnic table. My writing topic today was rescuing strays, not only Savannah but myself. I left a window and the door open so I could hear if she stirred. The girl had already proven she was a thief, and now I added *sneak* to her list of offenses. I didn't trust her, but I recognized the need for help. The first time I'd seen her, she'd been crying. She didn't look like the type to cry over nothing.

Just before dusk, a light went on inside the RV, and I hurried in to check on her. I didn't want her pillaging my stuff or, worse, sneaking out.

"You feeling better?" I deposited my laptop on the built-in shelf next to the TV. She'd folded the blanket and sheet and placed the pillow on top, making a neat pile on the couch. "I can make us dinner, if you feel like it."

She shook her head and pulled a toothbrush from her backpack. "Don't go to any trouble. If you don't mind, I'll brush my teeth and get out of your hair."

Any trouble? Who was she kidding? She'd probably given me a dozen more gray hairs, not to mention yakking in my bathroom. And I'd bought her two meals. Well, really one, since that waitress had seen a sucker coming when I walked in.

If she was so willing to leave just as it was getting dark, why had she snuck into the RV in the first place? My guess was shelter. I could only imagine how terrifying hitching rides could be. She'd pegged me as sympathetic when I bought her lunch. She'd probably seen me pull in—the RV wasn't exactly subtle—and saw a safe place to get her a few miles farther down the road. The only flaw in her plan was getting sick and blowing her cover. If nothing else, she owed me an explanation.

When she came out of the bathroom, I'd pulled a couple of frozen dinners from the freezer and was ready to pop them in the microwave.

"That's your idea of dinner?" she asked. "Those things will kill you with all the sodium. Not to mention they're loaded with preservatives."

"Like that burger, fries, and milkshake were much better."

"Yeah, you saw what that did to me, didn't you?" She slid the toothbrush into her backpack and slung it over her shoulder.

"Did you have something better in mind?" I didn't know a thing about this girl but realized I didn't want her to go. Something in her eyes told me she needed someone to talk to, and honestly, the miles had begun to get to me. Except for talking to the Bittners and Keith, I'd not had much conversation.

Her hand already on the doorknob, she hesitated. "You have eggs and cheese?"

I opened the fridge and produced a dozen eggs and a wedge of cheese. "What are you thinking?"

She dropped her backpack. "How about an omelet?" She pointed to the toaster. "Think you could handle toast?"

"Smart aleck!" We fell into an easy routine in the tiny kitchen. Savannah cracked eggs while I toasted bread.

Two omelets later, we were sitting at the table laughing at my burnt toast. "I don't cook much," I said.

"Really? I couldn't tell, not with all the junk food you have." Savannah forked a bite of omelet onto a piece of toast and pushed it into her mouth.

After we ate and washed and put the dishes away, Savannah grabbed her backpack. "Well, I guess I better get going. Thanks for everything."

"You can't be serious. We're in the middle of nowhere. It's getting dark." I folded the dishcloth and placed it over the edge of the sink. "Where will you go?"

She glanced outside. "Don't worry about me." She opened the door just as a bolt of lightning zipped across the sky followed by the low rumbling of thunder.

Part of me was relieved she was leaving. I'd raised my kids and didn't need another human being to take care of, and what did I even know about her? When another jagged bolt of lightning struck close by, the hair rose on my arm. "You're not going anywhere," I finally said. "There's plenty of room here. I'll make that couch back up, and you can stay here for the night." I shook the sheet and tucked it into the cushions. "I won't sleep a wink worrying about you." But would I sleep with her being in the next room?

"You don't even know me. Why are you being so nice, especially since I snuck in on you like I did?" Worry lines creased her young forehead.

"Yeah, well, we need to talk about that. Why did you sneak in here? Better yet, how did you sneak in?"

"You left the door unlocked. You seemed nice enough, and hitchhiking *is* scary. You never know what kind of creep is going to give you a ride." Savannah dropped onto the couch. "Normal people never stop. It's either the religious fanatics who want to reform you or the perverts who want to do you."

"And yet you're ready to go out there again?" I laughed. "Not tonight, young lady, and I'm neither of those, but then again, I'm probably not normal either." I grabbed a bottle of wine and a glass. "How old are you?"

"Almost twenty-one. I better not have wine just in case my stomach gets queasy again."

I uncorked the bottle and poured a glass. "I wasn't offering. And I don't believe for a minute that you're twenty-one."

"Really?" She eased back onto the couch and crossed her legs. "People always tell me I look older than I am. I hope it doesn't bite me in the butt when I get your age."

I choked on my wine. "Gee, thanks. Do I look that bad?"

Savannah laughed and held up her hands. "I'm sorry. I didn't mean it the way it sounded. You look great for your age."

I joined her on the couch. "You're just digging yourself deeper, so you better stop while you're ahead. Now, how old are you?"

"Almost twenty-one, for real." Savannah closed her eyes and yawned.

"I'm not going to press you, but I don't believe you. Just tell me you're over eighteen, because if you're not, we'll be having a totally different conversation."

She pulled a wallet from her backpack and displayed a Massachusetts driver's license, carefully covering her last name with her thumb, but letting me see her birthdate, which, after a quick calculation, I determined her age to be just a few months short of nineteen. That made me feel somewhat better.

"You're not even close to twenty." I patted her knee. "Get some sleep. It's been a long day."

I gave her a clean tee and a pair of yoga pants, and she stretched out on the couch. I gathered her dirty clothes, washed them in the sink, and hung them in the shower to dry. Monroe had a lot of amenities but lacked a washer and dryer.

While getting ready for bed, I called Kaitlyn and gave her the name of the park where I was staying.

"Can't talk now, Mom. I'll call you tomorrow." She disconnected before I could say another word.

It was just as well. If she had asked me what I had done today, I would have been at a loss for words. There was no way I'd tell her I had invited a stowaway to spend the night. My day sounded more like a made-for-TV movie than it did a relaxing vacation.

Just before I dozed off, I realized I hadn't heard from Tim.

CHAPTER SEVENTEEN

I was awakened by someone pounding on the door. It took me a while to orient myself, and my first thought was that the police had caught up with Savannah for something she'd done. I pulled on my robe and headed for the living room where I found her wide-eyed and armed with the pan she'd used for our omelets.

"There's some crazy dude out there screaming," she said.

I took the pan from her and approached the door. "Grab my cell phone and stand back."

Instead of standing back, she came close to my side. "No way. If he gets you, he'll have to get me too. We're a team."

Now wasn't the time to be a hero. I shrugged and pulled the window shade aside to see what kind of lunatic we were dealing with. I couldn't believe my eyes. I wanted to crack the lunatic over the head but put the pan away.

"What are you doing? We might need that," Savannah said, following me.

The pounding continued. "As much as I'd like to, I can't justify knocking my son in the head." I pushed the door open. Kyle stood there red-faced and huffing in the damp morning air.

"What in the hell do you think you're doing?" he yelled. "When Kaitlyn told me you'd actually gone through with this stupid idea, I got in the car and came over here to talk some sense into you."

Kaitlyn hadn't wanted to talk when I called last night, and now it made sense. She was playing Kyle's snitch. Again.

"Stop your ranting." I moved aside so he could enter. "Get in here before your asthma acts up."

He stomped inside, stopping short when he saw Savannah. "Who the hell is she?"

Savannah stepped back and grabbed the pan.

"Savannah, this is my son, Kyle. Kyle, this is Savannah. With the bad weather last night, she needed a place to stay."

He ran a hand through his thick hair. When Michael was Kyle's age, they could have passed as twins.

"You're taking in strangers? The next thing you know, you'll be telling me she's a homeless person you felt sorry for." Kyle looked from me to Savannah and back to me. "Mother, this is so not like you."

I hated to admit he was right. Old Annie would have ignored Savannah and certainly not bought her a meal, much less invited her to spend the night. But then old Annie would be sitting back home on her patio cursing the dandelions. New Annie had pulled every one of those suckers by the roots and then set out to find her new normal. "Stop it," I said. "She's not a stranger."

Kyle looked perplexed. "Kaitlyn didn't say anything about your traveling companion. Where'd she come from?"

"If you don't mind, I'm going to get dressed and leave you two alone." Savannah grabbed her backpack, fled to the bathroom, and shut the door.

"Honestly, Mother. Have you lost your mind? Do you even know the girl? She could be wanted by the police for all you know. Or worse." Kyle slammed his fist on the table. "And she's just a child!"

"Lower your voice," I said. "There's no need to scream. And who do you think you are, bursting in here like you own the place. You need to calm down."

He raked a hand through his hair and sank onto the couch. "I'm sorry. It's just—"

"You look tired. Let me make a pot of coffee." St. Louis was several hours away, so he'd been on the road for a while.

"I don't want coffee. I want you to turn this thing around and go home," Kyle said. "You have no business being on the road picking up homeless urchins."

"Stop it this instant. I'm not a five-year-old you can scold into behaving, and you are not going to browbeat me into going back to Florida." I jerked open a cabinet and pulled down a bag of coffee. A noise from the bathroom stopped me short. Savannah was sick again.

I dropped the bag. "Don't go anywhere. I'm not finished saying what I have to say, but I need to check on her."

She was huddled around the toilet again. I wet another rag and wiped her face. "Stomach at it again?"

She moaned and nodded. "Do you have any more white soda? It worked yesterday."

I poured a glass and shooed Kyle from the couch. "She needs to lie down. You and I can take our discussion outside."

After I got Savannah settled, Kyle followed me outside. We walked down the road and out of sight of the RV before I spoke. "Let me tell you something. I'm not a feeble-minded old lady you can push around, and I'm certainly not ready to sit around in a rocking chair making quilts and taking naps. Nothing is going to happen to me that I don't want to happen."

"But—"

"But nothing. Savannah is harmless. She's sicker than a dog, and I'm not about to turn her out while she's ill. What kind of person would I be?" Tears blurred my vision, and I blinked several times. "I'm on vacation and working on a new project, and I'm enjoying myself. For the first time in over thirty years, I'm doing something I want to do, and you aren't going to stop me." I took a deep breath and continued ranting, but I stopped when I realized he was laughing.

"What's so damn funny?"

"You," he answered. "I haven't seen you this fired up since you caught me and Larry Jamison smoking in the garage when we tried to convince you we were conducting an experiment for the science fair."

I stared at him. "Your tactic didn't work then, and it won't work now. I'm not going home. And it was rather dumb on your part to think you could strong-arm me."

"Crazy, huh?" Kyle leaned over and kissed my cheek. "I worry about you."

"I know you do. That's why I'm doing this. I'm worried about myself too. Since your dad died, I've been a shell of myself. Nothing interested me. Nothing brought me happiness. Even my friends have stopped coming around. I'm tired of living like that."

The rain ended, and a shaft of sunlight peeked through the clouds to the east.

"But it's all so sudden," he said.

"You have to trust me, Kyle. I raised you and your sister practically on my own. Lord knows your father wasn't around. I sat with you kids when you had earaches. I forced you out of bed on mornings when you stayed up too late reading comic books under your blanket with a flashlight. I've been a mother and wife for so long, I've forgotten who I can be. I need to do this."

I watched him out of the corner of my eye. His mouth was set in a straight line, not showing any emotion. "I'm stuck in neutral. I don't want to be in the same place next year or the year after that. If that's what you kids want for me, then I might as well move into the nursing home."

"You're checking in with Kaitlyn every night?" Kyle

asked.

"Yes."

"What's the deal with this girl? How do you know her?"

I explained how I'd met Savannah, omitting the part about her taking off without paying for her fries, the part about me getting stiffed for twenty bucks, and the fact that she'd snuck into the RV. That last part would really put him over the edge since I'd forgotten to lock the RV door. Basically, my watered-down story consisted of meeting Savannah at the café, her being sick, and me being concerned about her hitchhiking on her own. I might have fudged the timeline about her getting sick.

"Are you sure she's harmless and not a runaway?"

"Kyle, she's sick. I hardly think she's going to mug me in the middle of the night and take off with the RV. She could be a runaway, but she's not a minor, so technically I guess she isn't a runaway."

He didn't crack a smile.

"She had that opportunity to take off last night." I nudged his shoulder. "She's still here this morning."

His jaw relaxed and a smile appeared. "I'm not going to change your mind, am I?"

"No more than you and Larry Jamison did."

"You'll put her out if you have the least bit of trouble with her?"

"Yes." Or as soon as I got to the bottom of why she was hitchhiking in the first place.

Kyle scuffed a shoe in the gravel. "I guess you can't just abandon her."

"Absolutely not."

"Okay."

"Just to be clear, I'm not looking for your permission."

He hugged me. "You know I love you, Mom. I just want you to be safe."

I couldn't remember the last time Kyle had hugged me.

A softer side of my son had emerged, and I liked it. He wasn't the hardened man I'd thought he was. A glimmer of his once-tender heart shone through, and I not only loved the man standing next to me, but I also kind of liked him too.

Kyle squeezed me harder. "You're sure I can't talk you into going home?"

"No chance," I said. Old Annie would have packed up and gone home. Who was I kidding? Old Annie wouldn't even be here to pack up. My resolve was stronger than ever. Dealing with Kyle, I had overcome one more obstacle. At least temporarily. I rarely won with Kyle, but I'd take this as a win. I still had to make my peace with Tim. This confrontation made me more determined than ever to say what I needed to say to Tim. If we remained friends afterward, I would welcome it, but if we didn't, then he had never truly been my friend.

"I'm on a mission that I intend to complete. With or without your blessing. Now, I want you to go back to St. Louis and relax. If I can make it through raising you and your sister, I can make it through just about anything."

"You going to cook me breakfast before I hit the road?" He grabbed my hand, and we walked back to the RV together.

"Instant oatmeal or frozen French toast. What's your pleasure?"

"Your cooking skills have not improved, I see." Kyle laughed. "That doesn't have anything to do with the reason that girl is sick, does it?"

I frowned and punched his arm. "No, in fact, she made us an excellent omelet for supper last night."

"Too bad she's sick. I could do with an omelet. How about I take you to breakfast?" He slung an arm around my shoulder.

"You've got a deal. Let's check on Savannah. If she's resting okay, then we can go to the café in town."

The couch was empty. Savannah had folded the sheet and blanket. She and her backpack were gone.

CHAPTER EIGHTEEN

"Looks like your sick case flew the coop." Kyle sat in Monroe's driver's seat and whirled around. "This thing is awesome. I've always wanted to rent one."

"Don't just sit there. We've got to find her." I dug through my purse for my keys. "She can't have gotten far. Not as bad as she was feeling."

I tore out the door, hollering over my shoulder at Kyle. "Are you coming or not?"

"Let's take my car. I'll drive." Surprisingly, he hadn't wasted any time and was right behind me.

Before I could object, Kyle opened his passenger door. "Get in." He started the car and swung around in the gravel drive. "Which way do you think she went?"

"If you go left, that's the ferry into Kentucky. Let's go right. When we came in yesterday, there was a lot of truck traffic. She'll be trying to get a ride."

We drove several miles. Along the way, we passed a few homes, fields, and forest, and no sign of Savannah. Finally, he turned around and headed back to the campground. "It's no use, Mom. I think she's probably gotten a ride with someone."

My heart sank. I hated the thought of her getting in a vehicle with a stranger. She needed someone to take care of her, not take advantage of her. "Do you think we should call the authorities?" I sounded desperate, but I didn't know what else to do.

"What will you tell them, that you're looking for a hitchhiker you picked up? I think you need to accept the fact that she's gone." Kyle slowed for a tractor.

I shuddered and wrapped my arms around my shoulders. "If something happens to her, I'll never forgive myself."

"She's a tough kid or she wouldn't be out here. If it will make you feel better, we can at least call the sheriff. I don't know what good it will do, but it can't hurt."

When Kyle made the turn at the ferry road, I hollered for him to stop at the café at the end of the block. He screeched to a halt, and I opened the car door. "I'm going to check the restaurant. Maybe she's in there." I raced toward the café.

The place was packed. I searched the faces at each table, and my shoulders sagged when I didn't spot her.

Kyle caught up. "She's not here. Let's go back to the car, and I'll call the sheriff."

"Not yet. Let's ask around and see if anyone's seen her." A young couple at a table said they had just sat down and hadn't seen anyone fitting her description. Same thing with the next table. Kyle stopped two men on their way out of the restaurant and engaged them in conversation.

When a waitress came out of the kitchen, I hurried over. "Have you seen a young girl with long black hair?"

The waitress looked around and pointed to the empty booth by the door. "She was sitting there a while ago."

Relief flooded through me. "How long?"

She looked at a NASCAR clock over the front door. "Not more than five minutes."

"Hey, can I get a cup of coffee over here?" a man in a chambray work shirt hollered and pointed to his empty cup.

"Look," she said. "I got customers, and I'm the only one here. But that girl was here. Ordered a glass of water and then stalled. Kept looking over the menu like she was thinking hard. She didn't look so hot."

"I'm not getting any younger," the guy yelled again.

"Sorry, I got to go. Good luck." She rounded the counter, grabbed the pot, and sloshed coffee into his cup, causing it to run over and pool on the counter. "That quick enough?"

Kyle waved me to the front door. "The guys that just left said they thought she had gone to the bathroom and hadn't come out yet."

The bathroom door didn't budge. I pounded on it. "Savannah, are you in there? It's Annie. Let me in."

The toilet flushed, and I heard water running. "Savannah, let me in. We need to talk."

Geez, now I was the one saying it. I wondered if those words sent fear coursing through her like they did me.

Finally, the door opened a crack. That was all I needed to push my way in. Savannah retreated a step.

"Are you okay? I've been worried sick." She'd been crying again, and I wrapped her in a hug.

"Your son was so angry. I didn't think he'd understand." Sobbing, she sank to the floor. "You've got enough problems without worrying about me."

When I had pushed the door shut and locked it, I pulled a paper towel from the holder, kneeled beside her, and wiped her face. "Don't be silly. You scared us to death. Kyle drove me up and down the road looking for you. He's worried too."

Someone knocked on the door.

"Give us a minute!" I yelled. "Wash your face, then you're coming back with me. Do you hear? I'm not going to have you getting into some strange vehicle."

The knock grew more insistent. "Hey, I got to pee!" a woman yelled.

"Hey, it's occupied!" I shouted. "I told you to hold on."

Savannah blew her nose and wiped her face with another paper towel. "Even after all the trouble I've caused, you're still being nice to me. Why?"

Good question, but I couldn't turn her out like a stray kitten. "Because you need my help, that's why. And because I like you, Savannah."

"Really? You're not just trying to make me feel better."

"You're a very likable person. And you make a mean omelet. If you haven't noticed, I can't cook worth a damn."

"I—I like you, too, Annie." Savannah linked her arm through mine, then quickly pulled back like I'd slapped her. "Sorry. That was silly."

My heart broke. She acted like a puppy who had been conditioned to cringe at sudden movements. I pulled her into a hug, and she clung to me. "Savannah, it's okay, hon."

When the woman banged on the door again, Savannah pulled back. "Thank you for coming to get me."

I grinned and patted her shoulder. "Let's get going."

This time when she linked her arm through mine, she didn't hesitate or pull back. "Is my nose all red?"

"It sure is." I laughed and pulled the door open. "All yours."

The woman shot me a dirty look and pushed past us.

"Guess she had to go," I said to Savannah. "Now, let's find Kyle."

We opted to skip breakfast at the café and take Savannah back to the RV. After Kyle left with a belly full of instant oatmeal, I sat down with Savannah.

Her color and appetite had returned, so I made her toast and brewed a pot of jasmine tea.

We took our tea and the toast outside to a nearby picnic table. Savannah pulled a leg underneath her and blew across the top of her cup. We had made progress at the café, and I hoped she would feel comfortable enough to confide in me, but as skittish as she had been earlier, I didn't want to come on too strong. "Now tell me about Savannah. You're not trying to 'find yourself,' are you?" I made quote marks with my fingers.

Savannah dropped her gaze to the table and shrugged.

I had a hard time wrapping my mind around the fact that she didn't have a destination in mind, but then neither did I. Maybe we were more alike than I cared to admit.

"Look, I'm kind of in the same boat. Or RV as the case may be." I laughed, trying to add levity to our conversation since she was not forthcoming with information. "I have a general idea of some places I want to visit, but the truth is, the place I want to wind up isn't really a destination. It's more a state of mind."

She looked up from the table. "Like inner peace or something?"

"You might say that." I explained to her about losing Michael and how I'd been stagnant since his death. "I felt like I was running in place. Nothing I did made me feel better. I didn't even want to feel better. In fact, every little ache or pain sent me running to the doctor thinking, if I wasn't living, then I must be dying."

"How did you get here? Traveling in an RV."

I explained about getting the offer to write the article and how it coincided with my need to focus on what I wanted to do, not what everyone else wanted me to do.

"Like a reinvention?" she asked.

"You could say that. What about you? I know you're not

underage, so if you're a runaway, what are you running from? Are you in trouble with the law?"

"It's nothing like that. I promise. I needed a break and had to get away." She dunked a corner of toast into her tea.

At my age, I understood that, but she was so young. "Are you running from an abusive relationship?"

Tears filled her eyes. "Not really. I just needed space."

"I don't have to worry about the police showing up for you, right?"

She wiped her eyes with the bottom of her shirt. "No, I promise."

I sighed. Pushing her wouldn't get me answers any faster, and I'd already seen that she would run when backed into a corner. Until I could figure out her story, I didn't want to take that chance. I wanted her safe. If that meant giving her a little more time, then I would. "Okay, but we are going to talk about this. Understand?"

She nodded and whispered, "I know."

We sat there while she finished her toast and tea. When she pushed the plate away, I said, "Do you have a final destination in mind?"

"Not really. Just need time to think and get my thoughts together. Maybe decide what I really want."

"Kyle had to go to Europe after high school to find himself. My daughter, Kaitlyn, is still looking."

Savannah laughed. "It sounds like you might be trying to find yourself too."

That was almost the same thing I'd told Kyle this morning. "I guess I am. Pretty lame for a woman my age to be using that excuse, isn't it?"

"I don't know, it makes sense to me. Sometimes we get so engrossed in everyone and everything around us that we get lost in the shuffle."

"You're pretty wise for someone your age," I said. "You

seem to have a pretty good head on your shoulders. Except the hitchhiking. That's a pretty dumb thing to do."

Activity in the campground increased as RV owners began the ritual of packing up. I'd already decided to stay another day since the only schedule I had to meet was mine. Because of Kyle showing up and the cloudy morning, I'd missed the sunrise. That was on tomorrow's schedule. Today, if Savannah was able, we'd do a little sightseeing before I settled in to write.

"Look who's talking. You're the one who let a stranger into her RV and let her spend the night."

"If I remember correctly, I didn't let you in. I found you hiding in my bathroom." I sat back and studied her. The jeans she wore were faded and ripped—not in a rag bag sort of way, but in a name-brand way. The backpack she carried looked like it was made from expensive leather. She didn't put off a homeless urchin vibe. "Why are you out here, Savannah? A nice girl like you must have a home."

"Just wanted to see what the world had to offer," she said.

"Do your folks know you're hitchhiking?" She didn't wear a wedding ring, so I assumed there was no husband in the picture.

"My parents . . . Now, there's a question." She rubbed her hands together. "My mom is up to her diamond necklace in civic-mindedness, Junior League cookbook sales, and sleeping with her tennis pro. Dear old Dad is busting his ass on the golf course, schmoozing clients, and justifying why it's okay to get tanked before noon." Her words were drenched in bitterness.

"Sounds like you had an interesting childhood."

"You could say that." Her voice trembled, but her eyes remained dry.

I wondered what opinion Kaitlyn and Kyle held of their dad. They'd never uttered a word after his death, and I hadn't asked.

My kids could say a lot of things about Michael and me, but they could never accuse us of ignoring them. If anything, maybe I'd been a helicopter parent. Michael stayed involved where the kids were concerned, keeping up appearances. Once Kyle had made the break to Europe, I'd been hurt and disappointed and lost my connection with my son. Michael took it in stride.

"Parents never see the damage they do to their kids until it's too late." I'd felt an opening today in my interaction with Kyle. Our relationship wasn't entirely his fault. I'd been partly to blame, too, I supposed, for comparing him to his father. Part of my journey in finding myself meant putting back together all the pieces of my life that I'd disassembled or let slide over the years. I didn't have the opportunity with Michael, but Kyle was one of those pieces.

Even though I disapproved of her dropping out of school, Kaitlyn and I had maintained a good relationship. Probably because of her inability to stand on her own two feet and my inability to let her. Kyle, on the other hand, had landed on his feet and continued to disprove my assumption that him dropping out of school would result in failure.

Savannah nodded. "Let's talk about something else. This is depressing."

"You've got that right." I gathered our dishes and followed Savannah inside. "We are going to finish this, but for now I've got an idea, if you're feeling better."

"My stomach feels much better. That toast hit the spot, and anything sounds better than discussing my parents."

"Let's drive back to that town where the café was and see if we can find some touristy things to do. I wouldn't mind doing the ferry as long as I don't have to drive Monroe."

"You're on," Savannah said.

"First, I need to make a call." I took my cell and went to the bedroom.

Kaitlyn answered on the third ring. Music blared in the background. "Hello."

"Your brother stopped by today. You wouldn't know anything about that, would you?" The music faded, followed by a scuffling sound.

"Sorry. He called yesterday right after I talked to you, and I didn't know what to tell him."

"You could have told him to call my cell." Heat rose up my neck. Even though my conflict with Kyle had ended peacefully, it still irked me that she had ratted me out. Kyle could be overbearing, and he had a knack for pushing Kaitlyn around.

"You know how he is. I can't keep a secret from him. He's always been able to get me to spill the beans. How bad was he?"

"You know Kyle. He blew a gasket, but it passed. I'm surprised he hasn't called you."

When she didn't say anything, I figured he had, probably before he made it to the highway. "Kaitlyn, have you talked to your brother today?"

She hesitated, and I heard her fiddling with papers. "I got the college stuff today."

"I asked you a question. Did your brother call you today?"

"Yes," she said in an exasperated tone. "He did, and he said you had some girl traveling with you. I can't believe you of all people picked up a hitchhiker. If I had done that, I'd never hear the end of it. Don't you know how dangerous that is?"

"Stop it. We're talking about you and your penchant for buckling under to your brother. One of these days you need to stand your ground and not let him intimidate you. Now what were you saying about college?"

"I went to visit the admissions office today. Some of the stuff looks interesting. Classes start in mid-August, so I have time to think about it."

"Don't think too long," I cautioned. "Classes fill quickly,

and you don't want to get stuck with courses that won't do you any good."

"Good point. They have a hospitality major. They even offer a study abroad option."

"That sounds fascinating, but don't get too far ahead of yourself. Take it one semester at a time. You don't want to get overwhelmed."

"Tell me about this girl. Kyle said you found her at a diner or something. How old is she, and why is she hitchhiking?"

"Her name's Savannah. She's almost nineteen. I'm guessing she had a fight with her folks or her boyfriend and figured she'd leave for a while to let things settle down. She's been sicker than a dog. I couldn't just turn her out into the street. But as soon as I know she's better, I'm going to work on getting her to call her folks. In the meantime, I'm taking care of her. She seems like a good kid."

"Promise me you'll be careful," Kaitlyn said before we disconnected.

I promised, but the irony wasn't lost on me when I rolled my eyes.

CHAPTER NINETEEN

We found brochures in town listing all the interesting sights in the area. After riding the ferry into Kentucky, we visited an Amish community where we purchased local produce. In Marion, Kentucky, we ate lunch, then we headed north across the ferry and spent the afternoon hiking Rim Rock Trail in the Shawnee National Forest. It turned out, Savannah had an athletic streak, and I had a hard time keeping up with her, but I managed. By dusk, we were exhausted and called it a day. Savannah had a pink glow in her cheeks, but I could tell she was wearing down. Heck, I was wearing down.

"What shall we have for dinner?" I asked, rummaging in cabinets. "We could heat a can of soup, and I've got peanut butter and crackers."

Savannah scrunched her nose. "You've got to start eating healthier. How about I make salads with the produce you bought today. If you've got chicken breast, I could grill that for a protein."

"You make my heart sing, girl. What did I do before you came along?" I searched the freezer for chicken breasts but found none. "I have breaded chicken tenders."

"No way," Savannah said. "We'll both be wearing stretch

pants if we eat that way. A dinner of vegetables won't kill us. Wash those tomatoes while I tear the lettuce."

We discussed everything from politics to who our favorite bands were while we ate.

"You want to see if we can find a place to get mani-pedis?" I asked. "It seems we should be pampering ourselves."

Savannah blew a raspberry. "While I would love to have a mani-pedi, how about we do them ourselves? You can do my toes, and I'll do yours."

"You're on. I have everything."

After we'd cleaned up after dinner, I collected what we needed to do our nails.

Savannah wiggled her toes. "Let's do toenails first. Since we don't have a foot bath, we need to wash them good first, because I don't want you touching my grody feet like they are."

We took turns scrubbing our feet in the bathroom, and when we settled back on the couch, Savannah filed and shaped my nails.

"What's next for you, Savannah?"

She shrugged. "I don't know."

"You really don't plan to go home?"

"No."

"College?"

"That was a major argument with my parents. My grades were never high enough to get into the *good* schools, and since I was a hopeless case—my mom's assessment, not mine—it didn't make sense to waste their money. Again, my mom's assessment." Savannah closed her eyes and took a deep breath.

My heart melted. They had basically told their child that she wasn't good enough. When Kyle had shrugged off college, I remembered the screaming match he and I had. Michael had not gotten involved, but I sure did. I jumped in with both feet.

I patted Savannah's arm. "Don't for a minute believe that you are unworthy. You have value, sweetheart. Your mom was . . ." Her mom was what? A waste of oxygen? An inexcusable excuse for a human being? "Your mom was upset. I'm sure once she thought about it, she realized how wrong she'd been."

"Umm, no. She had a year to think about it, and her opinion didn't change. And my dream of culinary school evaporated." Savannah pushed cotton balls between my toes and applied the pearly pink polish I'd selected.

"Culinary school?"

Savannah smiled. "I've always dreamed of being a chef. Maybe even going to France, but Mom vetoed that idea. No child of hers was going to labor over a hot stove."

"That seems wrong. Has she heard of Thomas Keller or Gordon Ramsey and how successful they are?"

"I'm not sure what she wanted me to do, but I got tired of seeing disappointment in her eyes."

"What about your dad?"

"When my mom lays down the law, my father falls into line. The only thing he worries about is keeping my mom happy."

We switched places, and I gave Savannah her pedicure with a summery coral polish.

While we waited for our toes to dry, I tossed around an idea, weighing the pros and cons before airing my thoughts. It was probably impulsive. But taking the offer from Belinda and hopping in Monroe for the unknown was impulsive, so maybe I could channel that spur-of-the-moment girl I had once been.

When I'd decided, I said, "Are you game to join my trip?" I'd said it. No taking it back. Besides, it would give me more time to learn about her and her parents. We seemed to be getting along good, and if I could get her to trust my judgment, maybe she would see that calling her parents and mending their differences would be in her best interest.

Savannah's brows shot up. "Are you serious?"

I gulped. "I am."

"This is your journey. I don't want to be a burden. I can't even pay my way."

Was I being too impulsive? This girl was obviously wrestling her own demons. Did I need to inflict mine on her? Could I get where I needed to be mentally and physically if I took her along? Did I run the risk of taking on her problems as mine rather than letting her make her own decisions? No. She'd be back out on the road, and that would only endanger her.

I took a deep breath. "If you can keep up the gourmet cooking, I'll consider that your contribution." I rubbed my aching calves. "After the workout I had today, hiking those hills, and the healthy food you're putting on the table, I feel like I have my own personal trainer. I might even lose a pound or two."

Savannah threw her arms around me. "Then I'll consider that my challenge."

"Monroe is a no-whining zone," I said, wondering what I'd gotten myself into.

"You're on. High five." Savannah slapped her palm against mine. Her face lit up, and the change in her demeanor made me glad I'd invited her. She was slowly opening up, and she gave me something to focus on.

"Our next stop is Chicago." This was another place Michael and I had visited. I didn't know what I had been more excited about, eating at a fancy restaurant or watching my first baseball game in a major league stadium. The game had been amazing, but after sitting outside in the hot sun all afternoon, I was wasted by the time dinner rolled around. Michael's parents had made reservations for us and fronted the money for our meal. However, on the way to the restaurant, I had fallen ill, and we had to go back to the camper.

I knew this trip would not recreate that moment, but at least I could finally eat the meal I was so excited about all those years ago. Fortunately, the restaurant was still in business and under the management of the original owner's son. When I explained how I'd missed my honeymoon meal due to illness, they had gladly booked a reservation.

While I was in the bathroom, my cell rang. I quickly washed my hands.

"It's someone named Tim," Savannah said.

Had she just answered my phone? We'd need to have a talk about boundaries. I hurried from the bathroom and snatched my phone from the table.

"Sorry, I couldn't help but glance at the screen." She yawned and covered her mouth. "Who's Tim?"

My cell showed a missed call and no message. Savannah hadn't answered it, so I felt better about boundaries.

"A friend," I said.

"*Ooh la la*," she said with a French accent.

"No *ooh la la*. He was my husband's best friend." He *had* been my *ooh la la* at one time.

"Those are the best kind. Ask my mom. Best friends, tennis pros, fitness coaches. She doesn't discriminate." She yawned again.

"You look beat," I said. "Why don't we call it a night?"

She rubbed her eyes with the palms of her hands. "It's been a long day. Would you mind if I took a shower first? I feel like a grunge." She rooted through her backpack and extracted a toothbrush and a roll of dental floss. You had to like someone who flossed.

"Sure, there's shampoo, conditioner, and shower gel in there and clean linens in the cabinet over the sink."

While Savannah showered, I settled back at the table and debated calling Tim. Before I could weigh the pros and cons, a text arrived.

TIM: SORRY I MISSED YOU. CALL WHEN YOU GET A CHANCE.

I hesitated. Did I really want to call? Today had been emotionally draining. Talking to Tim would only dredge up the past. Maybe I needed that, needed to lay the past in front of me and cleanse it like dirty laundry. Or not. Before I could change my mind, I shot off a text to him.

ME: SURE.

The phone had barely rung when Tim answered it. "Hi Annie."

"Hi yourself."

"How's the trip? Any problems with the RV?"

"Good. No problems other than the driver." I laughed, stalling the inevitable. "I'm still a bit rusty, but I'm starting to feel more comfortable."

"Well, don't hesitate to call the dealer. Their number is on the visor."

"Right."

"What's your plan for tomorrow?" he asked.

Small talk made me crazy. No time like the present to jump in. My hand shook so hard, I could barely hold the phone to my ear. "Did you love me?"

"That's a silly question. You and Michael are—were—my best friends. Of course, I love you. Annie, I know I hurt you when I disappeared from your life. But believe me when I tell you how sorry I am. I'm hoping we can put this behind us and move forward. Pretend like I didn't lose my mind. Can we just do that, please?"

I thought for a moment. "I didn't ask 'Do you love me.' I asked 'Did you love me.' As in when we were dating. Did you love me then or was I just a diversion while you finished your studies?"

The line went quiet. I could hear television noise in the background, so I knew he was still there. "Tim?"

"I'm here. What—what kind of question is that?" Tim stumbled over his words. "We were kids."

Swallowing hard, I pushed ahead. "I think it's a legitimate question. Did you love me when we were together, or was I just someone to pass the time with when Michael wasn't available? A buddy?"

More silence, then, "Yes, Annie, I did." He said it so quietly, I could barely hear. "You were never just my buddy."

My chest squeezed. I felt like I was suffocating, but I was in too far to stop.

The bathroom door opened, and Savannah stepped out. "Oh, that felt so good." When she saw me on the phone, she took a step back. "Jeez, I'm sorry." She started to retreat into the bathroom, but I motioned for her to stay. Instead, I went into the bedroom and shut the door.

"You were determined to focus on an international journalism career. I had planned my career in intellectual property law. I couldn't ask you to change directions, and I couldn't change directions."

My heart raced as I tried to form a coherent sentence.

"I didn't realize that I loved you until I went home. When I came back to campus, you—you and Michael were together. I never dreamed the two of you would . . ." His voice trailed off into silence.

"Why didn't you tell me?" I asked. "What happened between Michael and me just happened. We didn't plan it." I wanted to blame it on the magic of the Barrister's Ball. I had felt vulnerable and a little bit drunk, and Michael was there. I had never thought about him in that way, until that night when he arrived at the dorm to pick me up. He looked so handsome in his tux, and I was smitten. And maybe a bit pissed that Tim had left and arranged a faux date for Michael and me. "Why didn't you fight for me?"

"When I came back to campus . . . I guess I was still in a daze after Mom's death. Seeing you and Michael together made me realize how stupid I had been for not telling you that I loved you. By the time I realized it, Michael announced that you were pregnant, and the two of you were getting married. What could I do then?"

His admission rattled me to the core. If I had known he loved me, would I have allowed myself to fall for Michael so easily? Would I have even gone to the ball with Michael? Would I have voluntarily given up an international career to stay home and write for the local paper? I did just that when Michael and I got married, but it wasn't really a choice. International journalism and pregnancy weren't terribly compatible. "I—I had no idea." The words stuck in my throat.

"I can't do this now. Can we talk later?"

Before I could answer, Tim disconnected. With my outlet for guilt retreating, I fell back on the bed and cried myself into a fitful sleep.

CHAPTER TWENTY

I had planned to wake up early and share a sunrise with Savannah before we left, but a storm rolled in during the night. I awoke in a crappy mood and in no hurry to drive Monroe over the curvy roads while it poured rain. I took two aspirins, went back to bed, and pulled the covers over me.

I'd had to shut the windows at some point during the night, but not before a chill invaded the RV. Lying there awake, I had nothing better to do than replay my conversation with Tim.

That thought did nothing but depress me. Should I have kept my mouth shut? We seemed to be making up for all the lost time since Michael's death, but maybe being impulsive would cost having Tim in my life. Instead of dwelling on the ifs, I needed to ditch my sour mood. I focused on my next stop in Chicago. We'd drive close to St. Louis, but since I'd seen Kyle yesterday, I did not intend to stop.

Had he not shown up, I still would not have, but since Kaitlyn had buckled under his pressure, at least my son and I had made peace. For how long, I didn't know. Not that I wanted to admit it, but it was probably a good thing that Kyle had badgered her into telling him where I was. Though, I didn't think so yesterday morning when he'd come barging in at the crack of dawn. In part, my showdown with Kyle may have fueled my need to confront Tim, which had resulted in a massive failure.

When the rain outside slowed, I rolled out of bed, hopped in the shower, and dressed for the day. Savannah was still asleep and showed no signs of coming to life. It was just as well. Deciding to let her sleep, I made all the preparations and tucked Monroe up for traveling. Just before I crawled into the driver's seat, I unstrapped Michael's urn from the passenger seat, carried it to the bedroom, and secured it. Then I woke Savannah.

By the time we hit the road, the sun was glistening off the wet pavement, sending steam into the morning air. I headed north, hoping for fewer curves than on the trip here, but that was not the case. I glanced over at Savannah who had buckled into the seat next to me and promptly went back to sleep. She sat up and pulled the blanket she'd brought from the couch tighter around her. I slowed down, but as big as Monroe was and with the grade of the road, all my efforts seemed to exaggerate the serpentine stretch of roadway.

"You okay?" I asked, focusing straight ahead. I'd seen several deer in the park and didn't want to wear one as a hood ornament.

In answer to my question, she unbuckled the seat belt and bolted from her chair. A few minutes later she emerged with a wet rag to her head and plopped down. "Sorry, I thought this would pass."

"Savannah, what's going on with you? How long have you really been sick?"

"It's nothing. I get carsick." She folded and unfolded the washcloth, then rolled it into a log that she held to her forehead. "These back roads are doing me in."

I wanted to pull over and make her look me in the eyes. When my kids were young, I could always tell when they were lying. I wondered what Savannah's tell was. Did she have a characteristic that only her mother knew? Scratch that. Savannah's mother probably wouldn't know. I stopped myself. I didn't know anything about Savannah or her parents other than what she had told me. For all I knew, her mother might be kind and gentle. At this very moment, she might be missing her daughter like crazy. That thought sobered me.

Savannah had curled into a ball and rested her head on her knees.

"You sure you're okay?" I prodded.

"Look, I get carsick. What is it with you?" she snapped.

I gripped the steering wheel and stared at the road. Was that her tell? Was getting short with me a sign that she was lying? Had asking her along been an impulsive move that would bite me in the butt?

The silence loomed around me. I turned the radio on, careful not to turn the volume too loud.

"It's okay," Savannah said softly. "I like country music."

I increased the volume and concentrated on driving. At the highway, I turned onto the entrance ramp and merged into the flow of traffic.

"I'm sorry I bit your head off," Savannah said. "I get grouchy when I don't feel good."

"No problem. I'm not much fun to be around when I'm feeling bad. I just worry about you. If there's something you're not telling me . . . well, I just want you to know that you can talk to me."

"Eww, don't get all *mom* on me." Savannah snickered. "Now that we're not on that roller coaster road, I'll be fine."

We passed the time playing the license plate game. I'd always played it on trips when I was a kid but never had the chance with Kaitlyn and Kyle—not with my we-can't-take-a-vacation husband. The kids and I did try on a couple of trips to the mall, but we were never likely to encounter more than two or three license plates different from our own. Kind of sucked the fun right out of it.

"There's a Missouri," Savannah shouted.

"It's the next state over."

"It's the first one we've seen, so I'm marking it down," she said, sounding triumphant.

As we neared Chicago, she was in the lead, and we'd spotted a whopping twenty-four different state plates, including an Ontario and a Hawaii, which diverted our attention while we discussed why a car from Hawaii would be in Illinois. Then we joked about getting seasick instead of carsick.

It was dark by the time we settled into our space. Setting up didn't take nearly as long with Savannah helping. She had searched the campground directory and found us a nice spot on the outskirts of the city. I had no desire to drive Monroe into the heart of Chicago. It was all I could do to keep him between the lines on the back roads we'd traveled. I sure didn't want to have to get into traffic and worry about changing lanes. He and I were getting along pretty good, but now was not the time to press my luck.

"What time are you going into the city?" Savannah asked. She had already opened the slide-outs and was making her bed on the couch. "I think I'm going to put a movie in and chill."

Before Savannah joined me, I had made reservations at the restaurant where Michael and I ate once. It had been such a splurge and way out of our price range. We were shocked by the menu prices, and had it not been for the generous gift card from his parents, we wouldn't have been able to afford it. We'd loved it so much that Michael had promised we'd go back when we weren't so financially strapped, but we never had.

"I'm not going," I said.

Savannah blinked. "Yes, you are. A nice night on the town is what you need. Relax and eat a great meal."

It did sound nice, but as I'd been reminiscing, I remembered how dressy the place was, and I didn't feel right leaving Savannah behind.

"I don't have anything nice to wear. Everything I packed was casual." I mentally ran through everything I'd packed—shorts, denim skirts, Capri pants, and jeans. Not one dress in the entire wardrobe, not even a dressy pants outfit. "I have an idea. How about we go shopping tomorrow? We'll take in the sights, hit a few stores, have an early lunch, and go there for dinner together."

"Together?" Savannah looked skeptical. "No, we can go shopping and see the sights, but tomorrow evening is yours. I'll stay here."

I grabbed her hand and pulled her off the couch. "Don't be silly. I'm not eating by myself. I'll call the restaurant and change the reservation to tomorrow."

Savannah's face crumpled into a frown. "Annie, stop. I can't keep taking from you. I can't pay my way. I don't mind earning my keep by cooking, but asking you to buy me dinner at a fancy restaurant is going way too far."

"Please, do it for me. I can't face it alone. If you don't go with me, I can't do it. Besides, one of these days you'll be a famous chef. Then you can be the one doing the treating."

She didn't respond right away. "I won't take no for an answer."

Her face brightened. "Okay, but I'm paying you back.

Every cent you spend, Annie Chisholm, I'm paying it back. I don't know how, but I'll find a way."

"Go put that movie in while I make the popcorn," I said.

Savannah danced her way to the television while I called the restaurant.

CHAPTER TWENTY-ONE

We spent the morning shopping along Chicago's famed Magnificent Mile. At Bloomingdale's, I found a navy cocktail dress with a simple line. It took longer to find something for Savannah. She pooh-poohed almost every dress, citing cost as an excuse.

I finally twisted her arm at Macy's where she found a stunning emerald green sheath that looked gorgeous with her long dark hair and fair skin. After we purchased shoes and bags to complete our outfits, we headed to the local deli for lunch.

The rest of the afternoon we spent touring museums, locating our restaurant for dinner, and walking the lakeshore.

We arrived at the restaurant promptly at seven and were escorted to a table overlooking the water. The setting made goose bumps rise on my arms.

"It's beautiful," Savannah said.

The view was perfect. I glanced around the room. Almost all the tables were tables for two. A young couple sat two tables over. She wore a sparkling diamond on her left hand and gazed at her fiancé with adoration in her eyes. To our left, an elderly couple held hands, their eyes locked on one another.

I ordered scallops and Savannah ordered salmon. The waiter suggested a wine to complete our meal, and Savannah held up her hand. "I'll just have iced tea, thank you."

Being a wine lover, I gladly accepted his suggestion. I always hated having to decide what went best with a meal.

Our dinner was amazing. I ordered another glass of wine and sat back in my seat.

Savannah pushed the asparagus around her plate and toyed with the salmon.

"Is something wrong with your food?"

When she raised her glass, her hand shook. Her eyes never left her plate.

I wanted to smack my forehead. "How can I be so dense? You're pregnant."

Savannah choked on her tea. "What?"

"You didn't have food poisoning and you weren't carsick. You're pregnant."

She pulled the napkin from her lap and wiped at a spot on the tablecloth. "Why . . . why would you say that?"

Fool that I was, I'd missed all the signs: the nausea and upset stomach, her lethargy, and now the wine.

"Don't play games." I signaled the waiter to collect my credit card. "Are you or are you not pregnant? And I want the truth." My voice sounded shrill, even to me. The diners around us stared. I wanted to crawl under the table and drag Savannah under there with me. The waiter hurried over and took my credit card. He'd probably process it in record time to get us out. It didn't look like the type of restaurant that appreciated conflict.

She cringed and slowly nodded. "Probably."

"How far along?"

"I don't know. A couple of weeks, maybe a couple of months."

I didn't need to ask the next question—I already knew the answer—but I did. "Have you seen a doctor?"

"No, I took a home pregnancy test. It was positive."

The waiter returned with my card. I signed the receipt and shoved the card in my purse.

"Let's go."

Savannah hung her head and followed me while I stomped to the car.

"Let me explain." Her voice wobbled. "You have every right to hate me. I hate myself."

I continued walking. "I don't hate you, but I don't want to hear excuses. You knew the first day I met you that you were pregnant. You should have told me."

By the time we reached the parking lot, my anger had traveled into the red zone. Savannah's deceit crushed me. I'd given her comfort, protection, and a home. I'd even bought her a damn dress, and she paid me back by lying.

We drove in silence while I seethed. When we reached the RV, I locked the Jeep, stomped inside, and threw the keys down. I left her standing in the living room and slammed the bedroom door behind me. My anger was too fierce to listen to what she had to say.

Sleep evaded me. Throwing off the sheet, I slipped on my robe and padded to the dark living room. Remembering how scared I was when I learned I was pregnant, I knew how Savannah was feeling. I suspected her parents had either kicked her out or she'd been too afraid to tell them. But what about the baby's father. Did he even know she was pregnant? Had he rejected her when she told him?

"Savannah," I called softly. I felt my way to the couch and kneeled beside it. "Savannah, wake up." When I got no response, I reached out to shake her, but she wasn't there.

"What the hell?" I flipped on the light. She was gone, her neatly folded linens a sure sign she had left. "Oh, for Pete's sake. Not again." I was too old for this crap.

My car keys were still on the counter. I grabbed them and headed for the Jeep. "This has got to stop," I mumbled to myself. This kid was making me crazy. I wondered if she was worth all the trouble. Here I was in mom mode again. Wasn't that what I was leaving behind on this trip? Not that I intended to abandon my role as a mother, but I had let being a mother and wife eclipse who I was as a person. This trip was supposed to be about finding that person in myself and freeing her to express her views and pleasures. That was why I had left Kaitlyn behind to sort out her latest dilemma with only a gentle push in the right direction. I couldn't live my life if I was busy living for everyone else. But I couldn't leave a pregnant Savannah to fend for herself. That dredged up too many memories of how my mother had rejected me. Had it not been for Michael, I didn't know what would have happened to me. I fired up the Jeep and went in search of Savannah. Unless I found her, I wouldn't be able to sleep.

Our campground was on the outskirts of the city. With any luck, the lack of traffic and the fact that it was the middle of the night would inhibit her ability to get a ride. I drove slowly, searching both sides of the road and watching for deer and other wildlife as I went. Not far from the campground, my headlights illuminated her figure sitting alongside the road on her backpack. I sighed, pulled next to her, and rolled down the passenger window.

"Get in," I said.

She crossed her arms over her chest. "No."

"Look, I'm sorry I yelled." A set of headlights flashed in my rearview mirror. The road had no shoulders and no place to pull off. "Come on, get in. There's a car coming."

She rose slowly and tugged the backpack behind her. I

recognized the "I'm doing it, but at my own pace" routine. I'd seen it in my son a thousand times over.

"Savannah, hurry before I get rear-ended." I turned on the emergency flashers, hoping the oncoming vehicle saw me before it was too late.

When she finally opened the door, the approaching headlights were so close, they lit the interior of my car. The blast of an air horn and chattering air brakes exploded in my ears. In a streak of yellow lights, a semi flew past me, rocking my car in its wake.

I gripped the steering wheel. "Get your ass in the car before we get killed!"

Savannah threw her gear in the back and crawled in. She'd barely buckled her seat belt when I floored the gas.

"That was too damn close for comfort," I said. "Were you trying to get us killed?"

"You're the one who stopped in the middle of the road. You should have left me here. I would have gotten a ride in the morning." She put the window up and leaned against the door, staring at me.

"You have to be the stupidest kid on this planet," I said. "When I was your age, I would have never had the guts to hitchhike, much less take off in the middle of nowhere."

"It sounds like you didn't have a lot of guts your whole life. Not until you decided to take this trip."

Her words stung, but I couldn't deny what she'd said. All my life I'd let other people control my destiny—my mother, Michael, my kids. "At first I thought going on this vacation was a really dumb idea. I mean, a woman my age traveling alone. What a stupid idea." Oh my gosh, those were almost the same words that Kaitlyn had said to me. "But then I realized I didn't even know who I was or what I wanted. My life revolved around sitting on my patio and eating chocolate. Do you know that until this trip I had never watched the sunrise?

All I had watched was the world pass me by. Good old Annie Chisholm, a yard ornament."

Savannah laughed. "You're hardly a yard ornament. I think you're brave. You almost got yourself killed a minute ago because you were too stubborn to go off and leave me. And driving that big old tank around is damn daring. I'd have the thing in a ditch in a minute. You drive it like a pro."

"My kids thought it was a lame idea, and when I was driving on those curvy roads the other day, I began to think they were right." My stomach knotted as I remembered how Monroe lumbered and swayed on those curves.

"Why'd you come after me?"

"Because I was mean to you. It's none of my business if you're pregnant," I said. "My feelings were hurt because you didn't tell me the truth. Besides I know what it feels like to be pregnant and scared. It just took me a while to realize that's what was going on with you." I pulled the car into a driveway and turned around.

"What did you have to be scared about?"

I told her about Tim and how he'd had to leave before the Barrister's Ball and had arranged for Michael to take me. "I got swept away the night of the ball. Michael and I both had too much to drink, and one thing led to another. Part of me was mad at Tim for leaving and going home. Another part of me rationalized that we weren't really in a relationship and that as soon as we graduated, we'd both go our own ways. We hadn't committed to one another. I hadn't realized how sick his mother was. She died shortly after he got home, and it was a couple of weeks before he returned to school." I turned in to our campsite and killed the engine.

"That's the Tim that called last night?"

I nodded. "By then Michael and I were a thing. And Tim never said a word. He didn't question me sleeping with Michael. The next thing I knew, I was pregnant and making rushed plans to get married."

"Wow! But everything turned out okay for you," Savannah said.

"Eventually. Kind of. But I still had to face my mother. I knew my dad would be hurt, but he'd understand. My mom was a different story."

We stepped out of the car, and Savannah came around and hugged me. "I'm sorry I didn't tell you the truth."

CHAPTER TWENTY-TWO

"Unpack that backpack and put your stuff in the overhead bin." I pointed to the cubby hole above the couch Savannah had been using as a bed. "The next time you get a wild idea to run away, maybe that will slow you down or at least I'll hear you."

While Savannah unpacked and remade the couch into a bed, I made hot chocolate and sat down at the table. "Tell me what you're afraid of."

"You name it." Savannah turned, and I saw the vulnerability in her eyes.

"Come and talk. I want to understand what's going on with you. Tell me the truth, the whole truth—not just the parts you feel like telling me." I patted the seat beside me. "I can't promise I can help, but I can listen."

Savannah slid into the booth and cupped her cocoa in both hands. "I don't even know where to start."

"How about the baby's father? Does he know you're pregnant?"

"No, I couldn't tell him." She blew across the top of the cup. "My mother doesn't even know we're together."

"Do they know you're pregnant?"

"Absolutely not."

"Sounds familiar. My mother had never met Michael before I told her we were getting married," I said.

"But at least he was a law student and had a future. Seth mows lawns. But he's hoping to open a lawn care and landscaping business," she quickly added.

"There's nothing wrong with that. At least he has a job," I said. An iota of what she said hit me between the eyes. I'd been the one to scoff at Kyle's decision to skip college and eventually go to work selling appliances. It had been me who told him he didn't have a future. Michael hadn't voiced an opinion. Now, Kyle was working himself up the corporate ladder. How wrong could I have been?

"Unless he's making a six-figure income and driving a Lamborghini, my mother would look down her nose at him. His mother is a waitress at a truck stop, and his dad works on a fishing boat. They are blue-collar all the way, and my mother is a royal snob."

"Mothers can be intimidating, but the important question is, do you love him?"

Savannah drummed her fingers on the table. "Yes, but it's way more complicated than that."

Nothing was too complicated if you loved someone. That had been my mantra when I finally got the nerve to tell my mother about Michael, though that was the least of my worries. There was a baby on the way. "The only complication I see is not telling him. Savannah, if you love him, and if he loves you, then it doesn't matter what anybody thinks."

"You don't know my mother. Not only will she go ballistic, but when she comes back to earth, she'll haul me off to some doctor and take care of this baby before I know what's happening. If I stay gone long enough, it will be too late for that."

"Listen to yourself, will you?" Remembering the day I'd told my mother about my pregnancy gave me a queasy feeling in the pit of my stomach. Not that I got the chance to tell her. I was poised to, but she knew before I'd said a word. It had gone downhill from there.

Savannah's bottom lip trembled.

"You're an adult for crying out loud. Not only that, but you're going to be a mother. You have a life growing inside of you. It's your responsibility to take care of it and nurture it. You're carrying your mother's grandchild."

"How did your mother take your news?" Savannah asked.

"You sure you want to hear?"

Savannah nodded.

"First, you have to understand that my mother was against me going to college. When I got my scholarship, she was beside herself. My mother had never worked, and she didn't understand my love of writing. She thought it was frivolous."

"That's my mom with me going to culinary school." Savannah drained her cup. "You want another cup?"

I nodded. "Michael went home with me, and we planned to break the news together along with the fact that we were getting married. The drive to Clear Lake was so stressful. The closer we got, the more my guilt set in. Michael was so sweet, but so innocent. He thought my mother would be understanding. I knew better. The first time I had brought a boy home when I was in high school was the last time. She grilled him within an inch of his life, including telling him there better be no hanky-panky. She scared him so badly, we never had a second date."

The microwave dinged and Savannah retrieved our cups. "I know the feeling. Only my mom lectures them about their pedigree."

"Michael quickly got on my mother's good side when he offered to help my dad fix the front steep, which my dad had been putting off for over a year. She even promised him a piece of apple pie."

Savannah smiled. "That sounds encouraging. Seth could walk on water, and my mom would still think he wasn't good enough."

I laughed. "It went downhill quickly. Dad and Michael had no sooner left for the barn to get tools than my mother told me if I had an announcement to make, I'd better get it over with. I had hoped to put it off until the next day." Tears pooled in my eyes, and I swiped them away.

"Michael and Daddy walked back in about that time, so I figured we'd better tell them. I asked them both to sit down. I grabbed Michael's hand and held on while I announced that we were getting married. Daddy didn't look surprised, but Mother . . . The look on her face. My mother had been raised on a farm and could sniff out a pregnancy with the best of them. Before I could tell them that I was pregnant, my mother made the announcement for me. That ended the conversation. She fled to her bedroom and stayed there the rest of the afternoon."

Michael and I had made peace with my pregnancy and were looking forward to becoming a family. But in one fell swoop, my mother had turned it into a tawdry affair with me being a scarlet woman.

CHAPTER TWENTY-THREE

Savannah and I moved to the couch with our cocoa, mine laced with Irish cream, hers plain.

"Wow, your mom didn't pull any punches, did she?" Savannah tipped her cup and took a tentative sip.

"No, I think she knew the minute I called her to tell here we were coming that I was pregnant. She made the rest of the weekend a living hell for me. If it hadn't been for Daddy and Michael, I wouldn't have had the courage to face her. The strange thing was that she really took to Michael. Made over him the whole time we were there. My dad did too. When they went to the barn for the tools, Michael had asked for my hand in marriage," I said. "Daddy thought it was nice that Michael had wanted his blessing, but he also knew a shitstorm was about to take place in the house."

Even though I was Daddy's princess, he always, always took the back seat to Mother when it came to discipline. Once she got on a roll, he never interfered, not even if he thought she was wrong. It was just the way Harold Buchanan was wired. Mother wore the overalls in the family, and Daddy did the heavy lifting.

"I don't have to worry about my mom liking Seth. She'll never give him a chance."

"What about your father? Any chance you'd get some support from him? Fathers usually have a weak spot where their daughters are concerned."

"When I was young, my dad would have done anything for me. Now, I don't know. He's too involved in his business deals." Savannah set her cup down and exhaled. "Maybe, I don't know. It's probably too late to build any kind of relationship with him. He's never around long enough to talk to. Not that I've tried lately. I can't blame it all on him. When my teenage hormones kicked in, I pretty much acted just the opposite of how my parents wanted me to. To say I was a brat is putting it mildly."

"Kyle and Kaitlyn were always giving me fits. Still do as you witnessed the other day. Regardless of how they act, I always loved them and would come to their rescue."

"Like your mom came to yours?"

"Touché. I see your point. My mother eventually came around." A knot formed in my throat, but I swallowed it. Now was not the time to get into that part of the story. "I don't think she ever forgave me for getting pregnant. But she did like Michael."

Savannah shook her head and squeezed her eyes shut. "It would take a miracle if that happened with my folks."

"What about Seth? Does he love you enough to stand up to your mother, enough to be a father to your baby?" I refilled our cups, adding a dollop of whipped cream to Savannah's and another shot of Irish cream to mine.

Savannah slowly nodded. "I think he does. I mean, he loves me, but my mom . . . wow, that's another story. He's a strong guy. He'd never let her push him around, but I don't even want to think about the two of them being in the same room."

"That's one thing I have to say about Michael. Despite all

his faults, he didn't back down when it came to my mother. He stood right by my side and didn't let her intimidate him. That's why I got the brunt of it. She knew he wouldn't bend, and she knew right where my weak spots were and zeroed in for the kill."

"That's what mine will do. Only she'll leave no witnesses," Savannah said.

"Honey, if you love Seth and you think the two of you can make it work, you owe it to yourself and your baby to try. The hell with your mom. She'll get over it or she won't. But either way, if you love Seth, you can't let your mom stand in your way."

Savannah leaned over and hugged my neck. "I wish you were my mom."

I hugged her and forced back tears.

"Now, tell me what happened the rest of the weekend with your parents."

"Not tonight," I said. "It's almost dawn. Let's see if we can get some sleep." I didn't have it in me to wait for the sun to rise.

CHAPTER TWENTY-FOUR

I slept until noon. The only pressing issue on my agenda was to get Savannah to a doctor. I didn't know how far along she was, but she needed a health assessment. If she wanted to keep this baby, she needed to be healthy and fit. I showered and dressed, leaving her to sleep.

I made two pieces of toast and smeared them with peanut butter and was contemplating our plan for the day when Savannah stirred.

"You want breakfast?" I asked. "I left you some milk, but I need to go to the store."

She raised her head and squinted. "No, I'm going to lie here for a while."

"Queasy?" I asked.

She waved her hand in a so-so motion. "It might pass if I don't move around."

"You want crackers or this?" I held up a triangle of toast. "I can make more."

She groaned. "Not yet."

"I was thinking that you need to see a doctor."

"Ack, you're sounding like a mom again." Savannah

pulled the blanket over her head. "I'll get back to you when I feel alive."

Popping the last bite of toast in my mouth, I shook the crumbs into the sink and rinsed the dish. She might not feel like it, but I would be in a better frame of mind once a medical professional proclaimed she and the baby were healthy. With that in mind, I grabbed my car keys. "I'll be back in a while." I let myself out and locked the door behind me. After our talk last night, I wasn't worried about her running again. She'd seemed agreeable, almost relieved, to accept my help.

The better part of the afternoon I spent locating a free clinic where Savannah could get a prenatal exam. I stopped at the local hospital and explained the situation. A nurse jotted down directions. An hour later, I turned the car in to a seedy neighborhood. My hopes fell when I saw gang graffiti. Almost every building had been tagged with some mark or another. Very artistic, but scary just the same.

I slowed the car and squinted to read the addresses. Three young men wearing baggy shorts lounged on the front steps of a brownstone. As I drove by, I noticed the address above the door was the one I was searching for. Fear clenched my stomach. I didn't usually venture far from my comfort zone, and this trip certainly stretched my nerves, but I needed to do this for Savannah.

Pulling to the curb, I exited the car and locked the door. I kept my eye on the pavement and made my way up the side-walk. When I got to the bottom of the steps, the young men parted and made way for me.

"No one's in there," a youth in a ratty gray T-shirt said.

I felt their eyes on me as I started back down the steps.

"Lady," another one called. "Don't leave. It don't open until three. Today's their late day."

"Oh." Glancing at my watch, I noticed I had twenty minutes until they opened. I started for the car.

"You don't have to leave," the T-shirted one called.

I watched in amazement as he spread a piece of newspaper on the step.

"You can sit with us." He grinned, flashing a brilliant smile. "We don't bite."

I hesitated. Nothing I'd done thus far fit inside my comfort zone. Why should this?

"Thank you." I sat down.

The young men quickly engaged me in conversation, talking up the clinic. It turned out they volunteered several hours a week doing office work, lawn care, and general repairs around the place.

Promptly at three, a perky blonde rounded the corner and threaded her way up the steps between us. Immediately she began giving orders.

"Derek, you're on trash and janitorial duties today. Raphael and Sammie, refill supplies and take turns manning the desk."

She stopped short when she saw me. Eyeing me warily, she asked, "Do you have an appointment?"

"No, but I was wondering if you have a minute?" I asked.

She jabbed the key in the lock and pushed the door open. "Come in. I have a few minutes."

Once inside, I explained the situation to her, and she put me at ease. She had Sammie pencil in an appointment for the next morning. At the very least, she could confirm Savannah's pregnancy, do an exam, and prescribe a prenatal vitamin. Once I talked Savannah into going home—*if* I could talk Savannah into going home—she could find an obstetrician to continue her care.

While driving back to the campground, my cell rang. I glanced at the display and saw Tim's number. Maybe it was because I'd shared my memories with Savannah or just felt lonely—I don't know what came over me. I pulled to the side of the road and answered. We had to finish our conversation, and before I chickened out, this seemed like a good time. I hadn't had a lot of time to consider our previous conversation or what I would say to Tim. I had been so angry at him for not fighting for me and then abandoning me when Michael died that I hadn't thought about his feelings. It was a miracle that Tim had remained friends with Michael and me at all.

"Hi." Apologies waited on my tongue.

"Sorry about not finishing our conver—"

"No," I interrupted. "I'm the one who owes—"

"Annie, stop. I need to say this." Tim's normally even tone was sharp.

"Go on." I deserved whatever he dealt. For all these years, I had held it against him that he hadn't fought for me, but never once had I even given a thought to the fact that I had been the one who caused our split—that I'd completely disregarded his feelings for me.

"I was angry at you and Michael after my mother's funeral. So angry. When Michael told me what had happened between the two of you, I wanted to punch him. But I didn't. He was so sincere, so apologetic. He even offered to stop seeing you if we could repair our friendship. But when I saw you and saw how happy he made you . . ." His voice broke.

I told myself to breathe. Part of me wanted to disconnect, but I knew I deserved whatever he was going to say.

He cleared his throat. "When I was home and saw how my dad tended to my mom, how much he loved her . . . Umm. This is awkward. Sorry. But I knew that's what I wanted. I wanted someone at my side who looked at me like my dad was looking at my mom. Someone holding my hand when it was my time. Annie, I realized I wanted you."

My throat tightened. "Tim—"

"No, I have to say this. Even though I was angry with both of you, I was angrier with myself for not saying anything to you about how I felt. But honestly, until I went home, I didn't even know. We had a good time together, but never once had

I thought about something more permanent. I figured once we graduated, we'd all go our separate ways. You off to some foreign country to report on third-world problems, and Michael and I to the law firms that hired us."

Tears streamed down my cheeks. "I'm so sorry. I'm so sorry." Those were the only words I could get out of my mouth, and I whispered them over and over.

"Shh. Don't cry," Tim said. "Please don't cry. This is not your fault. I think a part of me was scared to ask Michael to take you to the ball, but I think a part of me knew what would happen, and I was relieved because I knew you would be leaving, and I wouldn't have the guts to ask you to stay. At least not until I went home and had my revelation. It was a coward's way out. I was the coward, Annie, because I couldn't tell you that I loved you."

Tim's words reverberated in my brain. I swiped at my eyes, not trusting myself to speak.

"Are you still there?" he asked.

"Y-yes, I—I am." The words came out on choked sobs.

"When Michael finally told me you were pregnant, I was relieved. I knew he would give you a good life and that you'd be happy. Most importantly, you would still be in my life."

There was so much Tim didn't know. So much Michael and I had never told him. So much I needed to tell him.

Neither one of us said anything for what seemed like forever.

"Where do we go from here?" Tim asked.

"I don't know. I just don't know." The truth was, I still needed to level with him, but my emotions were swinging like a pendulum. Knowing that he had loved me all those years earlier, knowing that he had not been able to face telling me, knowing that he had let Michael and me create a life together without intervention, was something I needed to digest.

"If you decide you don't want me in your life, I'll understand, Annie. But I hope we move past the hurt. We used to be friends. I know I screwed that up, but I miss you. I miss Kaitlyn and her goofy dog. I don't know where we go without Michael in the picture, but I've been so damn lonely since he died. I need friendly faces in my life. I want to be able to see you in the grocery store and not feel guilty. Or call you when I need to hear a familiar voice. Can we press restart?"

"Tim, there is so much I need to tell you too."

"Nothing you can say will change my mind, Annie. It's late. Let's sleep on it. We can talk tomorrow. Okay?"

"Okay," I said. "I'll call you." I knew I wouldn't sleep. I would not be at peace until I cleared my conscience.

CHAPTER TWENTY-FIVE

Tim's confession had shaken me. Nothing had prepared me for what he said. All the ifs bombarded me throughout the night. If Tim's mom hadn't gotten ill. If I hadn't gone to the ball with Michael. If Tim had told me he loved me before going home. If. If. If. Sleep did not come. I threw the covers off, pulled on a pair of shorts and a tee, laced up my sneakers, and went out to the picnic table to wait for the sun to rise. Maybe in the light of day, I would find clarity.

"Annie, are you okay?"

I woke with a start to Savannah jostling my shoulder. "Huh?"

"Rough night?"

I nodded and stretched my arms in front of me, working the kinks in my back. I blinked to block the sun from my eyes. At some point, I'd put my head down on the picnic table and finally fallen asleep. Now I was paying for it with a sore back and aching muscles.

She set a cup of tea in front of me. "I heard you tossing and turning last night."

"What time is it?"

"A little after eight."

I rose from the table. "I need to shower. We have your appointment at ten."

Savannah tugged on my arm. "Are you okay?"

I tugged free. "I'm fine."

She shrugged. "I don't think so. What's bothering you? I heard you crying last night."

I exhaled long and hard. Savannah had finally been open and honest with me. Could I expect her to trust me if I didn't share what was bothering me?

"Come on, Annie," she urged. "I know something is wrong."

"My whole life is a lie. Michael and I weren't happily ever after. In fact, before he died, he could barely look at me. No one knew how miserable we were." I buried my head in my hands.

"Does this have anything to do with Tim?"

I nodded. "I have to tell Tim about Michael and me. About the sham we called a marriage. I cannot restart our friendship with a lie between us. It wouldn't be right."

Savannah rubbed my back. "If he's half the friend to you I think he is, he'll understand. How can he not?"

"You think?"

"All I know is that if he doesn't, then he was never your friend. And he doesn't deserve your friendship."

I took solace in her words and hoped she was right.

When we turned in to the clinic neighborhood, Savannah frowned. "Where are you taking me? This place is a dump."

"Don't worry," I said as I parked. "The nurse practitioner is very helpful. She has three neighborhood guys who help her. It's very safe, I promise."

Savannah followed me. A young woman named Karen greeted us.

"Come on back," Karen said to Savannah. She pointed to a stack of outdated magazines in the waiting room. "Make yourself comfortable. This will take a little while."

I sat in a faded vinyl chair and thumbed through a magazine, remembering my own experience at the campus health center. I had been terrified. Michael was so nervous, he couldn't keep his legs from bouncing while we waited for the doctor. The doctor, an old geezer, hadn't even tried to put me at ease. The whole experience had seemed more like an inquisition than an examination. In the end, the diagnosis, of course, was that I was pregnant with Michael's baby.

Savannah shook my shoulder. "Hey, are you asleep? I'm finished." She had a packet of papers clasped in her hands and a silly grin on her face.

"You're pregnant?"

"Yep, she thinks I'm about eight weeks."

"What now?" I asked, heading for the car. "Did she give you a prescription for vitamins?"

Savannah opened her door and slid into the passenger seat. I went around to the driver's side and let myself in.

"She gave me samples," Savannah said.

Now to convince her to go home and make things right with Seth and her mother.

After dinner, Savannah asked, "Where do we go next?"

I stopped drying dishes and turned around. "Not so fast."

Her eyes widened. "What?"

"Savannah, now that we know for certain you're pregnant, and it's not the flu or carsickness, you have to make a decision. You can't keep riding around the country. You need to get yourself home to a doctor and get regular medical attention so you and your baby remain healthy. Besides, I'm not going to be on the road forever. At some point, I'll be going home."

She perched at the table cross-legged. Her face clouded over. "I don't know what I'm going to do, and I don't want to think about it. Not yet."

I sat across from her and wiped at a spot on the table. "Look, if you want me to go back with you, just tell me. I'll turn Monroe around in a second. I'll be there when you tell your mom and dad. I'll be with you when you tell Seth. You have to tell me what you want to do because not doing anything is not an option." I patted her hand. "Do you understand?"

"I do. I promise. Just give me a couple of days to think about it." Her dark eyes searched mine. "Please. I know I've asked a lot of you, but just give me some time."

"Okay," I said against my better judgment. "But you've got two days. If you can't make up your mind in two days, I'm making the decision for you."

I had put Tim out of my mind all day. Or at least tried to. He had called once, and I had let it go to voice mail. Before I talked to him, I needed a clear head. That included sorting my feelings about what he'd said. I also decided to watch Michael's video. Maybe something Michael said in his video would give me clarity.

I retrieved the envelope from the bedroom and a glass of wine and went outside. Earlier I had set up my lounge, so I made myself comfortable. Savannah had found a movie on TV and was hunkered down on the couch with popcorn, so I had time to myself. The spaces on either side of Monroe were empty, and the RVs across the road were dark.

I slit the envelope and shook out the contents. A tablet slid onto my lap. A sticky note on the tablet read TURN ME ON. I waited for it to power on and clicked an icon labeled VIDEO ONE. My heart twisted when I heard Michael's voice.

The camera zoomed in on his favorite recliner—empty. Then he came into view of the lens and took a seat. I surmised the video had been made shortly after his diagnosis. The healthy glow of his complexion belied the disease raging within his body. Every hair on his head was still intact and combed to perfection.

After clearing his throat, he squared his shoulders and smiled into the camera. "I take it that Tim has been to see you. He's a good man, a real good man. I couldn't have asked for a better friend." He cleared his throat again and adjusted the camera lens to a wider angle. "Annie, there's so much I never said to you. There are probably things you wanted to say to me too."

"No shit," I said.

He laughed, the throaty melodious sound I used to love. "I can hear you now, ranting about the toilet seat. What is it with you women and the toilet seat? You got two hands. Put the damn thing down if you want it down."

Fair point. A couple of my friends who were also widows admitted that they got all teary-eyed when they walked into the bathroom now and the seat was down. Like it was an endearing quality about their spouse that they missed. Frankly I didn't miss the seat being up. No more worries about dunking my behind in the middle of the night when nature called.

"You're probably laughing your ass off. Can't say that I blame you. Poke fun at a dead guy. You probably found a million faults with me, but other than griping about vacation and the toilet thing, you never really acted like anything bothered you." In the background, his cell phone rang. "Be right back," he said to the camera. "Don't go anywhere."

He rose from the recliner, disappeared, and just as quickly reappeared and resumed talking. "Damn clients, it's bad enough they won't leave me alone at home. They can't even let me die in peace. Now where was I. Oh, yes. Bad habits, faults, stuff you didn't like about me. Want to know what I didn't like about you?"

I paused the video. The juxtaposition of the RV sitting behind me and my late husband getting ready to unload on my faults overwhelmed me. I wasn't the perfect wife, but he wasn't perfect either. Nothing like being angry at someone you couldn't argue with. Not that we argued when he was alive. He would have to have been available for a fight, and Michael was never available to me—even when he was at home holed up in his study.

I tapped play and said, "Give it your best shot, buddy."

"Your chili for one thing. Yep, your chili. It has no flavor. Beans and tomatoes with a bit of meat thrown in. Chili is supposed to be thick, not runny. Nasty stuff, but I ate it."

Seriously. He waited until he was dying to tell me he hated my chili. With everything else that was wrong with us, chili seemed rather trivial.

"And don't get me started about your vendetta with the damn dandelions. Annie, I'm rambling. This video isn't about our shortcomings, it's about my promise to you—the vacation I never gave you. I'm doing that now with Tim's help. Don't blame him, though. He's just carrying out my wishes. My last wish. I want to take that vacation with you—maybe not sitting in the driver's seat alongside you, but in your heart."

Tears welled in my eyes as I listened to my husband. Michael had always been in my heart, even when we were so far apart. I had never stopped loving him or hoping that we could find our way back to one another. But I had finally stopped trying because he had made it clear that we would never be the couple we had been.

"What drives a man to forsake his marriage? Power, money, greed, maybe some of those things. Quite possibly ego or the fact that I'm unforgiving. I see that now, but what's done is done, and I can't take it back. Just like your bad chili and the dandelions, it's something I can't bring myself to tell you face to face."

I knew where he was going. I dreaded where he was going, but I needed to hear it in his own words, because after the death of our son, our sweet precious Michael Junior, Michael had never uttered his name again, and he had never forgiven me for the accident that took our son from us. I had never forgiven myself.

For six years we had been the perfect family. Sure, it started rough. Two kids not ready for marriage were suddenly a family of three on a salary that barely put food on the table after the bills were paid. Michael worked fifty to sixty hours a week as an associate at the law firm he had interned with while he was in law school. I freelanced for the newspaper to make ends meet.

I felt like I had it all, though: a beautiful baby boy and a doting husband. And once a year a meager vacation hauling his parents' pull-behind trailer where we would dream of the day Michael made partner and our vacations could be more elaborate and exotic.

"I blamed you for our son's death, and that was wrong. The truth is, I wanted to punish you. It was easier to punish you for wanting to grasp a piece of your dream for us. Easier than it was for me to see that, while I had achieved *my* dream or was achieving *my* dream, you had put yours on hold when we had Michael Junior. I could not, without placing the blame on myself, justify the fact that your dream had been pushed aside to be a wife and mother." Michael coughed and cleared his throat.

He couldn't have punished me any more than I had myself. It had been selfish of me to expect to continue working after I learned I was pregnant with the twins, but continue working I did. By the time I reached my sixth month, Michael had begun a pressure campaign to get me to quit. I felt fine. My doctor said the pregnancy was progressing fine, and there was no reason I couldn't continue to work. Michael Junior had started first grade, so my days were free, and I loved working at the paper.

Michael reached for a glass of water on the table next to his recliner, took a drink, and continued, "Somehow in the privacy of my study, in front of the camera, it's easier to admit."

His words slammed into my heart like he'd hit me with a hammer.

"I always thought there would be time, that I would find the words to admit my failures. The more the years went by, the harder my heart became until we were so distant. You had hardened too. I don't know if it was grief, sadness, or just that you gave up on me. We—I never tried to reconnect and get back all the years we lost due to my stubbornness and negligence. Whatever my shortcomings, Annie, I always loved you. I loved our family. My grief blinded me to the important things and pushed you away. Maybe it's not fair for me to ask you to do this for me, but can you ever forgive me?"

The screen went blank. Everything blurred and my tears came, followed by sobs. I sat there for minutes, hours, I don't know, recalling the brief, usually curt, conversations throughout our marriage. Michael had never been a man for words, at least not outside the courtroom. But he had waited until he was dying to finally say the words I had longed to hear for years. And he asked for my forgiveness. Could I do that for him? For me?

CHAPTER TWENTY-SIX

A few days would buy me time before I had to deal with Savannah. When I began this trip, I knew at some point I'd find myself near Clear Lake. After the emotional night of watching Michael's video, I needed to see my mom. I knew going home would put me in an even more emotional state, but after all we'd been through, I needed her, which sounded strange.

Years ago, she would have been the last person I turned to for comfort, but we'd mended our relationship after Michael Junior's death, and she had mellowed. I had also changed from the straitlaced, innocent girl who left Clear Lake all those years ago. After four years at college without my mother breathing down my neck, I'd found my spontaneous fun-loving self only to have it kicked out from underneath me after my son's death.

The revelation that Michael hadn't blamed me for the accident did a number on me. If anyone could help me sort my feelings, it was my mom.

Before I'd watched the video, I had every intention of St. Croix Falls, Wisconsin, being my next stop. It had been another place Michael and I had visited. We'd loved the solitude and sheer nature of the area. I fully intended to go there, but not just yet.

"How about a detour?" We'd just left the campground.

Savannah had her shoes off and was painting her toenails fuchsia. She'd grown tired of the coral. "Where do you have in mind?"

"That's for me to know and you to find out." Despite my dour mood, I smiled and pressed the gas pedal. "Don't get that stuff all over the seat. This thing doesn't belong to me."

"You're such a worrywart. Quit being so bossy." Savannah went back to painting toenails, her tongue clenched tightly between her teeth.

"You won't be able to reach those toes in a couple of months. Enjoy it while you can." I laughed and headed toward Clear Lake and home. Or at least the home I'd known for the first eighteen years of my life. Four years ago, I'd been back for Daddy's funeral. Mother still had the farm but had leased most of the ground to neighbors. She'd kept enough to have a small garden and her orchard.

Savannah finished her toes and opened the map. "What highway are we on?" she asked, squinting at the fine print.

"You'll see when we get there."

She studied the map a while longer, scanning the road every so often, probably trying to catch a glimpse of a road sign. Finally, one came into view. She traced her finger along the map. "I know where we're going." She smacked the page with her index finger. "Clear Lake. That's your hometown, right?"

"Excellent deduction. One of these days you'll make a great detective. Until then, how about finding us some music?"

Our first stop in Clear Lake took us past the farm to a gravel lane off the county highway. When I pulled in under the wrought iron sign and parked, Savannah shot me a curious look.

"Why are we in a cemetery?" she asked.

"It won't take long. I've got something for my dad." I went back to my bedroom and pulled a bouquet of silk flowers from the closet. I'd purchased them a few days earlier, intending to take them back to Florida, but now that I'd detoured to Clear Lake, I decided they'd make a nice decoration for my father's grave.

I left Savannah sitting in the RV reading a magazine and made my way to the Buchanan family plot. The Clear Lake Cemetery had been around since the Civil War. The Buchanan section contained stones dating back to mid-1800.

Daddy's headstone was a double, with Mother's name and date of birth already engraved. Next to their stone was my brother, Kyle, who had died when he was an infant. I'd named my son after him. Next to Kyle, my father's parents were buried. And the line continued, one Buchanan after another.

In front of Daddy's stone, I dropped to my knees and pulled a few stray dandelions, careful to make sure I had the roots. Mother usually tended the family plot, but her arthritis made it nearly impossible to maintain it the way she wanted. Even though the cemetery had a caretaker, my mother used to make it a habit to pull weeds, place fresh flowers, and clean the stones regularly.

After I tidied the area, I removed the wilted bouquet and replaced it with the one I had brought. "Hey, Daddy, I brought flowers. Sorry they're not real, but they're pretty, and they'll last longer."

The air was still and quiet. Almost too quiet. I longed to hear the song of the summer tanager I'd grown to love as a child. Back home, I didn't hear many birds, most likely because I hadn't taken the time, but the tanager had always been my favorite. Its song was cheerful, almost kinetic with energy. A far cry from how I felt. I wanted that feeling. I longed for it. But my heart was heavy, and it felt like I was drowning and unable to catch my breath.

"Daddy," I started. "I've made so many mistakes. How do I know if I'm fixing to make another one? How do I undo all the years of unhappiness? How do I move forward?" I stopped and listened for the tanager. Still silence. The entire cemetery was quiet except for a light breeze rustling the leaves. I waited, knowing in my heart that my father would not be there to pull me close and ruffle my hair and tell me that everything would work out like he had when I was a child.

"I know everything that happened was my fault. Michael had every right to turn his back on me. I wanted to turn my back. I wanted to die, Daddy. I wanted to hurt."

I rested my head against the cold granite of Daddy's stone, hoping for a sign that I would be okay. That I could find the person I had once been. The sky clouded over and darkened. A testament to how I felt.

When the first raindrop fell, I got to my feet, brushed a few twigs from the top of the stone, and returned to the RV.

"Well," I said to Savannah. "You ready to meet my mother? She's mellowed now, but I'm telling you there was a time when she would have made your mom look tame."

Savannah brushed her hair into a low ponytail and fastened it with an elastic band. "Do I look okay?"

She'd changed clothes and removed the arsenal of earrings that lined her ears. Instead, she wore a tiny pair of gold studs. "You look great. How about me?"

"I think she's probably going to be so glad to see you that she doesn't notice what you're wearing."

I winked at her. "You're sweet for saying that, but I know better. She'll still scrutinize me. I'm sure she'll notice the ten pounds I've gained, the gray that keeps creeping in, and she won't like me wearing shorts. But we're past the bad stuff, and we accept each other for who we are."

Savannah sighed. "Do you think me and my mom will ever be at that place?"

"I'm betting anything can happen if you want it badly enough."

"And I'm betting if you step on the scale, those ten pounds are gone. You've been walking enough—that should have done it for you. Not to mention all the healthy cooking I've been doing." Savannah glanced nervously out the window. "Do you think she'll like me?"

"My mother? Sure, what's not to like."

"Uh, I'm pregnant. How's she going to react to that?"

"If you don't tell, I won't either. It can be our secret."

"Lucky for me I'm not showing." Savannah seemed to relax until I pulled onto the lane that led to the farm.

"Showtime," I said.

She took a deep breath and exhaled slowly. "I'll wait here. There's plenty to keep me busy. She doesn't even have to know I'm with you."

"Are you serious? Once she sees me drive in, she'll be in here in a heartbeat checking the place. You can't hide from my mother. I know that for a fact." I laughed and switched off the engine. "Come on, she's not so bad."

Mother was sitting on the front porch. She slowly got to her feet and scrutinized the RV. When I opened the door, and she got a good look at me, a smiled blossomed on her face. I crossed the yard, dodging raindrops, and was up the steps before she made it to the landing.

"Well, I never," Mother said. "What's that thing you're driving?"

"I'm glad to see you too." I hugged her neck and pecked her on the cheek.

"Well, I'm glad to see you. You're a sight for my tired old eyes. Why didn't you call? I would have had dinner waiting."

"That's exactly why I didn't call. You work too hard, and

besides, I might have a surprise for dinner," I said, hoping I could talk Savannah into preparing a nice meal for us.

I coaxed Savannah from the RV and made introductions. Mother led us inside and poured big glasses of lemonade.

She leveled her gaze at Savannah. "How far along are you, dear?"

Savannah choked and looked at me. "Ah. Well—"

"Mother," I said.

"Well, it's obvious the child is pregnant. I'm just trying to be polite and include her in the conversation. How is it the two of you are acquainted?"

Savannah looked to me again.

"She and I met awhile back." I didn't tell her that *a while* equaled a week and a half. "She loves traveling so I invited her along."

Mother rolled her eyes. "Surely you can manufacture a better story than that."

Leave it to my mother to cut right to the heart of the matter. "Well, if you must know," I started.

Savannah choked on her lemonade and sputtered.

"When Savannah found out she was pregnant, she left rather than face her boyfriend and parents." I chugged my drink and got a refill. "I found her sitting in a diner with nowhere to go and no one to turn to. It didn't seem right leaving her when I had this RV and nothing but time on my hands." How was that for blunt? If I expected Mother to blanch, she didn't.

Mother sighed. "Oh, Savannah, I'm sorry. I didn't mean to embarrass you." Mother patted her hand. "My daughter is a good person. You're in very capable hands."

Mother didn't offer compliments often and certainly not compliments about me. She had mellowed with age, and I loved the person sitting in front of me. I only wished she'd been this way when I was growing up.

Before Mother could prod Savannah for more information, I changed the subject. "What do you think of my rig?"

"It's huge. Where'd you get it?"

I explained how I came to be traveling in Monroe. "You want to take a look?"

Savannah popped in. "It's like a mansion inside, Mrs. Buchanan. Very plush and comfortable."

Mother waved her hand. "I'll have a look in a while. I need to keep my leg up."

I'd noticed when she met me on the porch that her leg was swollen. And now she had it resting on a kitchen chair. "What's wrong with your leg?"

"Just getting old. My circulation isn't what it used to be."

"Are you eating too much salt?" I asked.

"Probably. Everything is filled with salt, but I don't want to talk about me. Let's talk about Savannah."

Savannah's eyes widened. "Huh? We don't need to talk about me. In fact, I was going to go back to the RV and let you two visit. I know Annie's been dying to see you."

The little imp had only learned about our trip to visit Mother this morning. She certainly could spin a yarn.

"Not so fast," I said. "It's rude to drink your lemonade and run."

Mother homed in like a bee on pollen. "What was Annie saying about your young man? He doesn't know you're fixing to have his baby?"

Mother was nothing if not blunt. Thank goodness the years had eased her edges into soft curves or else I'd be running for the RV right along with Savannah. I hoped this visit would show Savannah that my mother had indeed softened her stance, the one that had driven me away so many years ago.

"No," Savannah said. "I didn't tell him. He's working hard to start his own business. Money is tight. I didn't want to add to his stress."

"Let me get this straight." Mother leaned in close. "You two are in love, right?"

Savannah nodded.

"What do you think he'd do if he knew about this baby?"

"Marry me, I guess, if that's what I wanted," Savannah said.

"Then you need to tell him, and the two of you figure it out. You have no business running off taking this man's child with you and him not know about it."

"That's only half the problem," I said. "Savannah's young man works for her parents, and her parents are rather well off."

"They look down their nose at him. Is that what I'm hearing?" Mother asked.

"That's putting it mildly." Savannah squirmed in her chair.

"You know Annie and I had words when I found out she was pregnant?"

"That's putting it mildly," I repeated Savannah's words. "We didn't speak for six years. Probably would have never spoken again if . . ." My throat tightened.

"Oh, Annie," Mother said. "That's water under the bridge. The important thing is we are talking. We'll never recover those missed years, but we have each other now." She turned to Savannah. "That's the lesson for you, young lady. Annie and I butted heads for years. We loved each other, but we butted heads. When she told me she was pregnant, I couldn't get past it. I felt I had failed her and that she had failed herself. If I had been able to see beyond my own pride, I could have reached out to my daughter. But she was just as stubborn. If she would have pushed, I would have backed down."

Savannah nodded in understanding. "You're telling me that whatever my mother says, I just keep pushing."

"That's exactly right. You show her that you're an adult,

not a little girl who needs her approval. If she sees you as an adult, then she'll treat you as an adult. You don't need her permission."

"Wow, I don't know if I can stand up to her. She's a tough one," Savannah said.

I shook my head. "No tougher than mine."

Mother crossed her arms and smiled.

CHAPTER TWENTY-SEVEN

I was up and dressed before dawn and made my way down the stairs. Mother had insisted that Savannah and I sleep in the house. She said it was cozier having us all under the same roof. I had to admit, sleeping in my childhood room, surrounded by all my familiar keepsakes, had been comforting. I still awoke feeling discombobulated and out of sorts. And probably would until I sorted all the mixed messages playing in my head.

Mother was already awake and sitting on the back porch with a coffee. I filled a cup from the old percolator she used on the stove top.

"Care for some company?" I pushed open the screen door and crossed the porch.

She patted the chair next to her. "Come have a sit."

I joined her and quietly sipped my stronger-than-mud coffee, silently cursing myself for not adding milk and a spoonful of sugar to cut the bitterness. The porch faced east, where the sun would rise directly over the far pasture, bathing everything in its soft glow.

Being a farm family, Mother and Daddy had always risen well before sunrise. By the time I rolled out of bed, their days were well underway, but the one thing they had always prided themselves on was watching the sunrise. I never quite understood the hoopla they made. At least not until I began this journey.

No matter the time of the year, Daddy would already have his barn chores well underway, and Mother her household chores, but the minute they sensed the sun beginning to peek above the horizon, they'd stop what they were doing and meet on the porch. Once the sun had made an appearance, they'd go their separate ways and continue their daily chores. I had to wonder if Michael and I would have lost our way if we had made the time to enjoy a daily ritual such as beginning our day together.

"What's on your mind, child?" Mother set her cup down and scooted her chair around to face me.

Even though I had come home to get my mother's advice, I hadn't expected to have the discussion quite yet. But I should have known she would see into my heart and suss out my feelings long before I'd figured out what I wanted to say. It was ironic that I was about to spill my secrets to her when, years ago, she was the last person I would have sought advice from. She had been judgmental, and I had been unwilling to listen.

My son's death was a turning point in my life. I had lost my precious child, and in the process, Michael's blame had turned him against me. And me against myself. But my mother—losing a grandson that she barely knew had changed her. Had changed her attitude toward me. Where once she was cold and unforgiving about my pregnancy and the subsequent birth of my son, she instantly became the mother I had always longed for. The years of judgment and disapproval fell away as she comforted me in my time of need. It was odd to me that, as horrid and unspeakable as Michael Junior's death had been, my mother had risen to the occasion. Our entire relationship changed the day of the funeral.

"Annie, I've got nothing but time, so we can sit here all morning if you want."

"I have so much on my mind. It's hard to know where to begin," I said.

Mother bent forward and put her hand on my knee. "You remember when you used to help me weed my flower beds?"

"Help is stretching it. More like you forced me. I would have preferred doing anything to weeding. I hated digging in the dirt and getting it under my nails."

"If you had worn the gloves I gave you, it wouldn't have been a problem."

"Yes. I learned that lesson but not quickly enough. You used to get so mad at me for just jerking them out of the ground." I winced at the memories. After every rainfall, I could count on Mother dragging me out to the yard to help her tidy the beds.

"You just made more work for us when you did that. If you leave the root, the weed just comes back and continues to spread. You have to dig the root and all." Mother took a long sip of her coffee. "Problems are like that, too, Annie. You can't just pinch them off. You have to go after the root of the problem. Dig deep to get rid of it.

"You remember that whole bed of creeping phlox you pulled? I had spent hours planting that, and in one afternoon, you managed to dig up every one."

"How can I forget? You still remind me. See, if I had pinched them off, they would have come back, and we wouldn't still be talking about them," I teased.

"True, but if you had identified them before you went to town, we also would not be sitting here talking about them. And you would have saved yourself a lot of work. If I remember correctly, that bed was in pretty good shape and shouldn't have taken long to tidy up. But you took the whole afternoon."

I laughed. "Yes, and you were so angry."

Mother's brows knit together. "Do you get where I'm going with all this garden talk?"

"I think so. I need to identify my problems, then tackle them one by one, getting to the root of each problem."

She touched her nose with her finger. "Bingo. You're feeling conflicted. I can sense that. Honey, after your father died, it was all I could do to get out of bed each morning. If you're feeling out of sorts because of Michael's death, it is totally understandable. You found your way after you lost Michael Junior. That will happen again. Trust me."

"That's just it, Mom. I never found my way after his death. To this day I still blame myself. I still carry the guilt with me. If I hadn't insisted on working, if I hadn't made the detour to cover a story on the way to taking Michael Junior to school, he would still be here." I covered my face with my hands as my emotions rushed back.

Mother pulled them away. "Listen to me. That accident was not your fault. Another driver ran the stoplight. You did everything you could have. Your baby was strapped in his car seat. You protected him as much as humanly possible."

"But he's still gone. If I had driven straight to school, we would not have been near that intersection. Michael knew that. That's why he turned against me. All because I was stubborn and put my job ahead of my family." Tears streamed down my cheeks.

Mother pressed a tissue in my hand. "Dry your tears, child, and tell me what this is all about."

I began with Tim dropping off the RV, then went on to tell her about writing the article for Belinda's new magazine.

Mother sighed. "I don't understand the problem. You've apparently taken Tim up on the RV, and if I know you, you're already working on the article or at least contemplating what you're going to write. There's more to this. We've got plenty of time."

I sucked in a breath. "Mom, I'm miserable. I've been

miserable for years. When Tim dropped off the RV and Belinda offered the job, I thought I could find the old Annie. To begin to rebuild my life. I know life will never be normal—at least not the normal I've been used to—but Mom, I want normal. I want to look in the mirror every morning and like who I see. I want to love myself again. I want to look forward to a new day." I stopped and blew my nose. "Do you know, a couple of days ago, for the first time since I can remember, I watched the sunrise. Just sat and watched it come up. I found the magic for a moment. It dawned on me, literally, why you and Daddy always took the time to watch it together. I want that magic every day."

"We're fixin' to see it ourselves." Mother pointed to the pasture. "It's just beginning."

"Michael left a video. He made it after he got sick."

Tears came to Mother's eyes. "I would give anything to have a video of your father. Just to hear his voice one more time."

I had sat at my father's grave and wanted to feel his arms around me and his words of comfort. Why couldn't I find comfort in Michael's video? In his words? "He told me he had wrongly blamed me for Michael Junior's death. That it was his fault that he couldn't let it go and had taken it out on me. But I blamed myself, so why shouldn't he?"

"Honey, I know you keep reliving the accident over and over in your mind. But it was an accident. A tragic accident. You can't continue to blame yourself for someone else's actions. Michael lashed out at you, and he told you he was wrong to do that. You will never be happy and never be able to move forward until you stop blaming yourself."

I knew she was right, but it was so damn hard.

Mother scooted her chair closer and took my hand. "Look at the pasture."

I raised my head, and the sun spread a glorious light over the pasture. The dew that had fallen earlier sparkled like a million diamonds had been dropped from the heavens.

"It's glorious, isn't it? I always feel closer to your father when I watch the sunrise. And I tell him everything on my heart." She leaned over and kissed my cheek. "Try that with Michael and Michael Junior. And love yourself, honey." With that, she got to her feet, collected our empty cups, and padded back into the house.

I pulled my robe tighter, stepped off the porch, and headed to the pasture. My slippers were soaked by the time I reached the fence that surrounded the pasture. When I was little, Daddy would sit me on the top rail while he worked. I'd sit there for hours watching as he mowed or raked or baled the hay. I always felt at peace watching him do chores. I climbed up on the rail, hoping that I still had the flexibility to get myself seated without falling on my face.

"Michael Junior," I started, realizing that I had never once talked to my son since his death. Maybe it was because I was too ashamed of myself or guilt-ridden or that I was unworthy of telling him how much I missed him.

I cleared my throat and started again. "Hi baby. It's Mama. I miss you so terribly much. There isn't a day that goes by that I don't think of you and see your sweet face." I sniffled and pushed away tears. "Your daddy and Grandpa Buchanan are with you now. Always remember that Mama loves you. And Michael, if you're there, take our son's hand and keep him close. He needs you. And me, well, I'm working on me. Knowing you're with our baby and taking care of him will help."

I closed my eyes and squeezed them tight, waiting for a peaceful feeling to come over me. In the distance, I heard the whistle of the train crossing Main Street in town. A light breeze tousled my hair, and the scent of grass surrounded me. I waited.

"Michael, you asked me in your video to forgive you. I've

thought long and hard about that. How can I not forgive you? We were both at fault, and if I can't forgive you, then I can't forgive myself." I sniffled and looked across the pasture. A rasp found its way into my words. "I have to forgive myself. I know it won't be easy, but then nothing ever has been for us, has it? I'm making myself a promise today with you and our son as witnesses. I promise to try and forgive myself. No, I do forgive myself. I won't ever forget the tragic day that took our son's life, but I will stop accepting blame. Michael, I forgive you. I forgive us."

In the distance, I heard the faint chirping of a bird. It grew louder and more insistent. I recognized the song of the summer tanager and opened my eyes.

Sitting on a rail not thirty feet away were three tanagers. In that moment, I knew what to do with Michael's ashes. I'd take them back to Florida and spread them over our son's tiny grave. A feeling of peace descended over me like I hadn't felt in ages. My legs had gone numb from sitting, but I couldn't make myself leave. When the trio had finally flown away, I climbed down from the fence and went back to the house. Despite wet feet, I felt warm all over.

CHAPTER TWENTY-EIGHT

Mother and Savannah were at the stove. I stood in the doorway and listened to them chatter. Savannah was giving Mother tips on preparing low-sodium meals that tasted good. I didn't want to interrupt the moment, so I returned to my chair on the porch and pulled my phone from the pocket of my robe.

Tim's voice was coarse from sleep when he answered.

"I'm sorry if I woke you," I said.

He cleared his throat. "No, don't worry about it. I needed to be up anyway. Where are you?"

"We're at Mother's."

"We?" Tim asked with a note of concern in his voice.

I smacked my forehead. "Yes, I'm surprised you don't know about her. Kaitlyn ratted me out to Kyle. I assumed she'd told you too."

"We've talked, but she never said a word about a traveling companion."

"It's no big deal. It's a young woman I met along the way." I explained how I'd met Savannah and how she'd reminded me of myself when I was her age.

"You be careful." Tim's protectiveness warmed my heart.

"I am. You don't need to worry."

He sighed. I could almost see him raking a hand through his hair.

"It's all good," I said. "It's been a while since I've seen Mother, and I wanted Savannah to meet her. Savannah's mother and mine have—no, had—a lot in common."

"Ah, the old hard-shell exterior with the soft center." Tim laughed. "The one that you needed a chisel to break."

"She's not like that anymore," I said.

"I know."

"About our call the other day." I lowered my voice so Mother and Savannah wouldn't overhear my conversation. "I've been thinking a lot about what you said."

"Me too. I shouldn't have said anything."

"No, I'm glad you did. I've been so full of myself. I needed to hear what you said. But I need to tell you something." If I confessed about my and Michael's relationship, I ran the risk of alienating Tim once and for all. He had been Michael's friend long before he'd been mine, and it might be that he wouldn't understand, or maybe he'd blame me for the marriage breaking down, but I was done accepting blame.

"Annie, we don't have to rehash our past."

"But I do. You need to know about Michael and me. We were not the perfect family. Everything you saw, everything the public saw, was a facade. Michael and I barely talked." I took a deep breath, hoping I could get through this. I needed to unload this before I imploded. I needed to dig the hurt out by the root.

"After Michael Junior died, Michael blamed me. He could barely look at me. I could barely look at myself in the mirror." I gripped the phone so hard, my knuckles hurt.

"*Blamed* you. Mic—Michael blamed you for the accident?" Tim's voice quivered. "Annie, that can't be right. The accident wasn't your fault."

"He blamed me for not quitting work when I found out I

was pregnant with Kyle and Kaitlyn. I was taking Michael Junior to school the morning of the accident. Right before we left, my editor called me and asked me to go to the courthouse because the jury was coming back with a verdict on the Kline murder case. If I hadn't been going to the courthouse, we wouldn't have been at that intersection."

"That's ridiculous. Michael never once indicated to me that he blamed you."

"Exactly, the only person who knew how deep his blame went was me, and I wallowed in it. Do you remember the day of Michael Junior's funeral?" Michael's words had been so harsh that morning. I was paralyzed with grief and so pregnant with Kyle and Kaitlyn that I could barely move. Tim had come to the bedroom to check on me after Michael had already left for the funeral home. Tim was so kind, so empathetic. When he had pulled me to him to comfort me, I had practically thrown my pregnant self at him. He must have thought I had lost my mind.

"Yes. Annie, it's all in the past. Why are you telling me this?" Tim asked.

"I finally watched Michael's video." It dawned on me that Tim had helped Michael with the video and had probably been there when Michael was making it. "You probably already know what he said."

"Michael had me set up the camera, but then he asked me to leave the room. The next time I saw it, the tablet was already in the sealed envelope. I didn't open it."

"He told me he didn't blame me for our son's death. He waited until he was dying to tell me. We lived a miserable existence for all those years with him barely acknowledging my presence. And I continued to dig myself deeper into grief and guilt." I shifted in the chair and pulled my robe tighter.

"So, what does that mean for you now?"

"Good question. I guess I take it one day at a time. I know the grief will always be with me. My son will always be a part of my past, part of my life. I can never put that behind me. I don't want to. But I have to move past the hurt and guilt that I have piled on myself with Michael's help. If I don't do that, I won't ever have a new normal. Mother made me see that."

"It sounds like you're getting some closure," Tim said.

"It won't happen overnight, but this morning I had sort of a breakthrough. I talked to Michael and Michael Junior this morning. Don't take that the wrong way. I don't mean in a wacko, talking-to-the-walls sort of way. But I let my heart talk. I have never been able to do that. And afterward, I felt more peaceful than I've been in years."

"It sounds like this trip is turning out to be a positive thing. Are you able to do any writing?"

I laughed. "I started on a roll, but I've slowed to almost a halt the last couple of days. But I need to let today simmer a bit, then I'll get back to it. I'm also working on getting Savannah reunited with her parents. But it's all part of my journey, so I'm sure I'll find a way to include her in my writing."

"Annie, do you think . . ."

I waited. When he didn't finish, I said, "Think what?"

"Nothing. Never mind."

"Don't do that. Don't start a sentence and then leave me hanging." That was a classic Tim move.

"Do you think we can hit reset?"

My pulse kicked up a notch. What was he asking?

"I know you have a lot of issues to work through, getting yourself back on track, but I'd like to help. I recognize that I played a big part in your dropping out. I should have been there for you, should have been there for the kids, but I guess I had to face my grief before I could do that. Can we? Can we get our friendship back on track and start over?"

"I'd like that." For the second time today, I felt like a giant brick had been lifted from my shoulders.

"Breakfast is ready!" Savannah hollered from the doorway.

"You go eat breakfast. We'll talk later," Tim said.

I felt so at peace at Mother's that we spent three more nights there. I told Savannah that just because I had extended our stay didn't mean I had forgotten about her calling her parents. I hoped that being around Mother would show her that it was possible to mend her relationship with her mother.

Savannah cooked like a demon and filled Mother's freezer with low-sodium meals she could pop in the microwave. Mother took Savannah to the barn where she dried the herbs she grew. Savannah was ecstatic when Mother allowed her to select a variety of herbs to take with us. In the evenings, Mother pulled out the dreaded family photo albums, and we all shared a laugh at my expense. Mother even agreed to take a ride in the RV, which she declared was *okay* but not nearly as comfortable as her Cadillac. It was the best time I had ever spent with her.

The night before I had planned to leave, Savannah called her mom. I didn't overhear the conversation, but afterward, Savannah stayed in her room and didn't emerge until well after I had watched the sunrise with Mother the next morning.

Mother left us alone on the porch with the excuse that she was going to make breakfast.

"I take it your talk with your mother didn't go well?"

Savannah pulled her knees against her chest and hugged them. "You could say that."

"Did you tell her about the baby?" I asked.

Savannah shrugged. "Nope, didn't get a word in over her shouting."

I took her hand. "Maybe she needs time. How about your

dad? Do you think you could pave the way with him? Maybe you can get him to talk to her."

A tear rolled down Savannah's cheek. "Maybe. I don't know. She usually runs right over him."

I handed her a tissue from the box Mother had brought to the porch for me.

"Mom told me if I was hell-bent on leaving, then I could just st-stay gone." Savannah's voice hitched.

What kind of mother did that? Mine probably would have had I not gone away to college and grown an independent streak. I certainly could not imagine her welcoming me and a baby back home. Had Michael not asked me to marry him, she probably would have packed me off to live with my spinster aunt in northern Minnesota. "She can't mean that. She's just hurt. You need to tell her about the baby, honey."

She took a swipe at her eyes and squared her shoulders. "No, absolutely not. She was stone-cold serious. I'm not going back. At least not until my pregnancy is further along. If it means I get a job, then that's what I'll do. I could find something at a café and maybe get a room somewhere."

The girl had a stubborn streak too.

"Really? You think you can handle medical bills and room and board on the wages from being a short-order cook or a server?"

She buried her face in her knees and sobbed.

I kneeled next to her and rubbed her back. "Look, we have to figure this out, but I'm not leaving you in the middle of nowhere. We have a little more time, but we are going to hash this out, even if I have to call your mother myself."

Savannah straightened. "You can't do that, please. That will only make it worse. Promise me. You don't know her."

"I'm not making that promise. Does she even know where you are?"

"She said she doesn't care where I am and not to call her

asking for money. She said when I grew up, I could come home."

That left me in a quandary. We couldn't stay here at Mother's indefinitely. I could already tell our visit was wearing her out. She wasn't used to the excitement of company and having people underfoot.

I had planned to get Savannah on a plane home once she had made peace with her folks and then head up to St. Croix Falls, but I couldn't do that until I knew she had a home to go home to. Otherwise, I was sure when the plane landed, she would be back on the highway hitching a ride to who knew where. I couldn't take that chance. I decided to take her along while giving her mother a few days to cool off. Once a few days had passed, I'd convince Savannah to give her mother another call or at least get in touch with her father.

CHAPTER TWENTY-NINE

The morning we left, Mother wrapped her arms around Savannah and me and said a prayer for our safety on the road. She had insisted we stay a few more days, but I could tell her plea was not sincere. She looked tired, and she had been favoring her left leg. Still, she had insisted on trying to wait on us despite our attempts to lighten her load by cooking meals and cleaning up after ourselves.

After Savannah had seated herself in Monroe, Mother stepped close and whispered, "How was the call to her mother?"

I frowned and shook my head. "Didn't go well. I'm going to give her mom a few days to cool off, and then if Savannah won't call her, I will. She needs to be back home."

With tears in her eyes, Mother hugged me again. "You're a good person, Annie. Take care of yourself and let me know what happens."

"Mother, are you sure you're okay?" I asked, hugging her one more time. I worried about her and had queried her numerous times, but she assured me her doctor had everything under control.

"I'm fine, honey. I just got my annual checkup a couple of

weeks ago. Doc Cooper said I was fit as a fiddle. Told me I needed to lose ten pounds, but he's been telling me that for twenty years now."

"Well, maybe with your leg swelling like it is, you should take his advice."

Mother laughed. "That's a role reversal. You notice that *I* did not bring up weight. Now you're doing it."

I had held my breath since I drove in waiting for my mother to make a comment about my weight or the gray in my hair. "I'm sorry. But I worry about you."

"I know you do, but I'm fine, really. Fit as a fiddle, remember?" She swatted my backside. "You better get on the road before the traffic gets bad."

We had planned a slow travel day of sightseeing on the way to St. Croix Falls. Savannah had taken a highlighter and marked all the spots along the way where we should stop.

"Did you talk to Tim last night?" she asked while she marked our map.

I told her about talking to Tim and the possibility of restarting our friendship. She listened with the ear of a good friend, nodding in the right places, and not offering much in the way of commentary.

"Uh-huh," I said, staring straight ahead.

"Sounds like more than friendship?" She continued to draw, not looking up.

"What? No, just friends."

"But you dated him before Michael."

"That was a long time ago," I said. "A very long time ago. It was more like hanging out than dating. We were different people then; a lot of water has gone over that dam."

"But you have to admit it sounds promising. There are

stories on TV all the time about people reconnecting with their first loves after they've raised their families."

"We were never serious," I said. "Strictly platonic."

"Maybe *you* weren't. He could have been before Michael staked his claim. Maybe Tim just moves slower."

"No, he admitted he worried that taking our relationship to the next level might scare me off due to my future plans. He backed off after Michael made our announcement, and we didn't test the chemistry again for a long time, not until the day of my son's funeral when I practically threw myself at him, and he turned me down flat. No, I'd say that ship sailed a long time ago."

"Well," Savannah said, "you won't know unless you board the ship, will you?"

I nearly choked. "I can't believe you said that. Tim's my husband's best friend."

"Your late husband," she corrected. "You're not dead, Annie. It's time you wake up from your fog and decide what you want to do with the rest of your life. Taking this trip is a first step, but honestly, you need to get a life."

I bristled at her impertinence. "You don't know what it's like." But if I was honest with myself, I *had* begun to wonder if there could be something more with Tim. I knew I couldn't erase all the years with Michael, and I didn't want to. But I also wanted to think there could be happiness in my future, and that future would look a whole lot brighter with Tim in it.

"No, I don't. But I'll tell you one thing. I'll be damned if I sit around watching the grass grow underneath my feet."

"Isn't that exactly what you're doing?" I asked. "Why are you out here instead of moving on with your life? Why haven't you contacted Seth? It looks to me like you need to take your own advice."

Savannah crossed her arms and blew out a breath. I could tell she was exasperated, but no more than I was. I continued to stare at the road.

Finally, she threw the map on the floor. "I can't stand arguing with you. Sometimes you act just like my mother, and it makes me want to scream."

Her immaturity had surfaced. "Well, that would be a real grown-up thing to do, wouldn't it?"

Savannah screamed a wicked scream that echoed throughout Monroe.

I swerved, and Monroe's right tire went off the pavement. My breath hitched as I jerked the wheel, fighting to pull us back onto the road. We crossed over into the oncoming lane. Monroe fishtailed and wobbled. I gripped the wheel and fought to get us back into the proper lane. Had there been traffic, we surely would have been killed or killed someone.

None of my practice runs had prepared me for a catastrophe like this. When I finally returned to my lane and straightened the big RV out, sweat ran down my face in rivers. My arms ached from the stress. I took a deep breath and searched for a place to pull off and get my wits about me. Every muscle in my body shook and twitched.

When I saw a farm implement store ahead, I put my turn signal on and pulled into the lot.

"What the hell was that all about?" I demanded.

Savannah's face had gone pale. Her arms were wrapped tightly around her belly, and her breathing came in gasps. "What the hell, Annie?"

"What the hell, indeed! You could have killed us screaming like a banshee."

Cursing under my breath, I unhooked my seat belt and exited the RV. When my feet hit the ground, I wanted to drop to my knees and kiss the pavement. Instead, I bent and put my hands on my knees, taking in deep breaths until I stopped shaking. I did a circle check of Monroe to make sure none of the tires had blown and that the Jeep was still attached.

When my pulse returned to normal and I wasn't afraid that I would throttle Savannah, I stepped inside and took my seat. I dared not look at her for fear that I'd let her have it. I calmly turned the radio on and tuned it to a country station. Carrie Underwood's "Jesus, Take the Wheel" was playing.

Savannah started giggling, then burst into a fit of hysterical laughing. "That seems appropriate."

"Stop it," I said. But she kept right on cackling until tears ran down her cheeks. "It's not funny."

"The . . . timing . . . of . . . that . . . song . . . is . . . perfect." Her words spilled out between guffaws. She couldn't control her laughter, and soon, she had me laughing too.

When she got herself together, she said, "I might have screamed, but you're the one who drove all over the highway."

I suppressed a giggle. "I did that because you scared me. I almost peed my pants."

"I did." She stood up, and her shorts had a definite wet spot. "I better go change."

Savannah and I spent three days traveling the north shore of Lake Superior. We stopped at waterfalls, lighthouses, and even dipped our feet into the chilly waters of *gichi-gami*, the Ojibwe word for *great water*, better known as Lake Superior. I told Savannah about the Gordon Lightfoot song "The Wreck of the Edmund Fitzgerald," and the poem "Song of Hiawatha" by Henry Wadsworth Longfellow. Both of whom had pronounced it *gitche gumee*. She showed me how to download the song onto my laptop.

Every morning I woke before dawn, and while I waited for the sunrise, I meditated and let my heart open and talked to my son and husband. I no longer spoke the words but allowed my thoughts and memories to wander. The guilt and gloom slowly began to melt away, and slowly I sensed an inner peace that lasted longer each day.

At night after dinner, while Savannah read, I worked on not one piece for Belinda's magazine, but I had spun that one idea into several. The exhilaration I felt at doing something creative filled me with excitement. I had sent one of the pieces to Belinda, and she'd suggested a couple of changes, but overall, she was thrilled. Even more thrilled when I told her I had several more ideas.

Savannah and I had long talks while we were seeing the sights. She had told me more about Seth, and I had opened up about Tim. Since he'd made his admission, we had begun talking every evening, trying to sort our friendship. Things were still rocky, but we were headed in the right direction. I felt certain that by the time I returned to Florida, we'd get back to some sort of a new normal for us. I wasn't quite sure what that would look like, but at least I looked forward to seeing him again. In fact, I looked forward to a lot. I had jotted down a few more ideas for my novel but didn't want to take it further until I had finished the articles.

We were heading south on Interstate 35 just south of Minneapolis.

"I can't wait to read something you've written. I've never known an author before."

"I'm not an author yet, but maybe one day after I finish these articles, I'll write a novel." My articles were practically writing themselves, and I couldn't wait to get the last one finished and turned in so I could get to work on a book. The novel idea had practically taken control of my brain, and I had to tamp it down to work on the articles.

"You could make your main character a chef." Savannah clapped her hands together. "That's it. She could own a five-star restaurant overlooking Lake Superior. No wait. It's probably too cold in the winter. She should be on a beach in Florida. Or better yet a tropical island."

I laughed. "Great idea. Keep going. We may have to co-write this novel."

"She's known for her creativity and wit." Savannah beamed. She continued to list recipes the chef would be known for.

"Would that chef be you?"

Her face fell. "No, I'll be living in my parents' basement raising a baby, hoping for my knight in shining armor to get his business off the ground and then free me from the dungeon. I'll probably have to sell lemonade on the sidewalk to pay for diapers and formula until that happens."

I had begun to see a new level of maturity in her. She had agreed to call her parents when we made our next stop and to call Seth after her conversation with her folks. During our long talks, we had discussed the fact that my trip would be winding down and that she would have to decide.

"Stop it." I swatted her arm. "You, my friend, are looking at the glass half-empty. You assume you know how your parents will react. And maybe you do have a history with them, but they might surprise you. You won't know unless you talk to them. And when I say talk to them, I mean talk to them as an adult."

Savannah groaned. "Easy for you to say."

"You know I'm speaking from experience. I didn't take control of the situation when I told my mother, so she already had the edge. I just hung all my insecurities out there. If I'd had a plan to show her I was headed in the right direction, my outcome would have been different. She even admitted as much." That statement made me shiver. A plan was exactly what I needed now to change my outcome. I hadn't reinvented Annie way back then, but I felt like I was well on the way now.

CHAPTER THIRTY

We were just outside of Iowa City visiting the Amana Colonies. Savannah had promised to call her parents tonight, and I had taken her for a day of shopping. With as many baby clothes as I had bought, you'd have thought I was the grandmother-to-be. Savannah and I trudged into the RV, arms loaded with shopping bags.

"I can't believe you bought all this stuff," Savannah said, pulling a plush yellow teddy bear from one of the packages. She nuzzled it against her cheek. "You'd make a fantastic grandmother."

"Ah, that will be the day. Kyle's job is all-consuming. He can't take time for a wife, much less a child. But it's probably for the best. Kaitlyn, on the other hand . . . well, maybe one of these days." I smiled, thinking about the possibility. "In the meantime, you're still calling your folks, right? You promised. In a week, I'll be going home, and I'm not going to feel good until I know you've made peace with your folks and that you have someplace to go."

Savannah curled her lip. "I promise."

"No time like the present. You need to start getting regular medical care." I pulled my cell phone from my purse. "It's not going to get any easier."

Almost in slow motion, Savannah dropped the bear and clutched her abdomen. The color drained from her face.

I rushed to her side. "What is it? What's the matter?"

She crumpled onto the couch. "Something's wrong. It hurts."

An hour and a half later, I was sitting in the emergency room while the doctor on call examined Savannah. Thoughts whirled through my head. If she lost this baby, I'd never forgive myself for not insisting that she call her folks sooner. I put myself in her mother's shoes and thought about Kaitlyn being on her own, pregnant, and scared. How would I feel if she had turned to someone else because she couldn't confide in me?

Approaching footsteps caught my attention. A doctor coming down the hallway walked toward me.

I rose from the hard plastic chair. "I-is she okay? Baby? Is it? Did she lose the baby?" The words came out in a jumble.

He rolled his shoulders as if from fatigue. "She's fine. The baby's fine. We're going to run some tests and keep her overnight," he said. "She's anemic and may have a urinary tract infection. We'll get some antibiotics into her and get her a prescription for a prenatal vitamin. Has she seen an ob-gyn?"

My hands shook and relief surged through me. I explained that Savannah had seen a nurse practitioner and that I was trying to convince her to go home to Seth and her parents.

"She's not handling the stress well, so if I were you, I'd do whatever it takes to see that she takes care of herself. More importantly, I want you to get this prescription filled. She needs to be taking vitamins." He pulled a pad from his pocket, scratched across it with a flurry of his pen, and handed me the paper.

"Can I see her?" I asked, placing the prescription into my purse.

"She's resting, but you can go on back."

I started to leave, but his hand on my shoulder stopped me.

"Get in touch with her family. If she's going to carry this baby to term, she needs to be home seeing a doctor on a regular basis."

Savannah was curled up with her eyes closed when I walked in. She looked so young. I leaned in and tucked a strand of hair behind her ear. "How are you feeling?"

She opened her eyes, a tear sliding down one cheek.

"Hey, you're okay. The doctor said the baby's fine." I sat next to her and gently rubbed her arm.

"I know, but I'm scared. It didn't seem real, you know, that I was going to have a baby, until I worried I was going to lose her." She placed a protective hand on her abdomen. "I want this baby more than anything, and I'd never do anything to hurt her."

"Her?"

"Well, the doctor said it's too early to know she's a girl, but I'm not going to keep calling her *it*. But a boy's okay too."

"Good for you," I said. "I'm going to call Seth and your family. Your mom might surprise you. And if she doesn't . . ." I took a deep breath and exhaled. "I'll be there for you. But only if you try with your mom first."

Another tear slid down her cheek and soaked into her hospital gown. "Since I told you I would call her, that's all I've been thinking about. It's been fun driving around in Monroe with you, but I know I've got to do what's right for my baby, and that means growing up." She reached for a tissue and blew her nose. "I can't grow up unless I can face my parents. I want my baby to have a whole family. If Seth and I are meant to be together, we can take whatever my mom dishes out like you and Michael did. If we can't, it's better to find out now."

She had a hard time ahead of her. I'd had Michael next to me when we told my parents. If Savannah didn't have Seth to turn to, she'd have no one.

"I'm going to call your mom," I said.

"Let me talk to Seth first," Savannah said. "Then you can call her."

CHAPTER THIRTY-ONE

The next morning, the doctor came in and told Savannah that all her tests had come back in normal ranges and that she was free to leave. That put a smile on her face and mine.

"Young lady, if you take care of yourself, there's no reason you can't have a healthy baby." He took her hand in his. "But you have to start by being a healthy mom. Take your vitamins, exercise, and eat right."

Savannah blushed. "I will, I promise."

After getting her buckled into the car, I headed to the nearest pharmacy. "The doctor said we have to fill a couple of prescriptions. Why did you tell me you had samples of prenatal vitamins?"

Savannah blanched. "The clinic gave me a prescription, but I didn't have the money to get it filled."

"I would have paid for it," I said.

"I know, but you've done so much already. There is no way I'm going to be able to pay you back."

"We've had this conversation." I pulled into the pharmacy and dropped off the prescription. When I returned to the car, we agreed to go to breakfast while we waited for them to fill the prescription. After the waitress had taken our order, I leaned back in the booth. "How did your talk with Seth go?"

A smile formed on Savannah's face. "At first it was hard. He was mad because I'd left without telling him anything. He asked me to come back to see if we could work things out."

"Did you tell him about the baby?"

"Not yet." Savannah fiddled with a napkin, tearing off small bits and then wiping them into a pile.

"Savannah—"

"Wait," she interrupted. "I'm going to tell him, but that's not the kind of news I can deliver on the phone. I want to see his face when I tell him. It's easier to read expressions in person."

That's exactly the reason I hadn't said anything to Savannah's mother when I talked to her last night. I'd told her about Savannah being in the hospital but left out the part about the baby. That was Savannah's news to deliver.

Our food arrived, and Savannah dug in like she hadn't eaten in a week.

"What?" she asked, her mouth full of pancakes. "I'm eating for two. The doctor said I need to maintain my strength."

"Riiiiiight," I said. "You eat like that, and you'll be waddling to your first appointment."

She grinned and stuffed another forkful into her mouth.

"I talked to your mom last night," I said.

Savannah's fork froze in mid-air. "Yeah?" she mumbled. "Let me guess, I'm cut out of the will. Or worse, I'll be banished to a convent where I'll have the baby in secrecy, so her society friends won't know." She poked the fork at me. "Abortion is not an option. She can go straight to hell. This is my baby, and I'm keeping her."

I swirled my coffee and took a sip. After a while, I said, "I didn't tell her you were pregnant."

"You didn't?" She seemed surprised.

"That's your responsibility. I'll support you and stand by your side, but that's something you have to tell your parents yourself." I motioned to the waitress for a coffee refill.

"I'd rather have a tooth pulled—without anesthetic."

I hesitated. I had to tell her. At this very moment, they were boarding a plane. "Um, Savannah."

"Yeah."

"We're having company this afternoon."

"She's coming here?" Savannah glanced over her shoulder.

"They both are. Their flight gets in at three," I said. "I offered to meet them, but they decided to rent a car."

"Wh-wh-what did they say?"

"Don't worry. Your mother was very nice. We had a long talk. She's worried about you."

"Yeah, I'm sure." Savannah snorted. "Probably worried she'll miss her tennis lesson."

I pushed my plate away. "Come on. We can talk about it on the way to get your prescription."

Savannah sat on the couch, covered with an afghan I'd brought from the bedroom. She'd picked nervously at the edge until she'd worked a thread loose.

There was a chill in the air, and I'd brought two cups of tea and sat next to her. "It's going to be fine. Your folks will be supportive. Maybe not right away, but trust me, Savannah. If I had tried harder all those years ago, maybe I could have prevented the rift between me and my mother. Once she shut me out, I backed off and didn't try. Now, I know that if I had kept after her, we could have mended our differences much sooner."

Tiny wisps of steam curled off the cup Savannah held. "I don't know if I can do this, Annie. I've never been able to stand up to my mother. She's like this larger-than-life persona. Everything about her is perfect. Perfect life, perfect house, perfect marriage. At least on the outside. Then there's me. I don't fit the mold. When she enrolled me in ballet, I was a klutz. At school, I didn't excel at anything. The only skill I possess, the one thing I really love doing, she deems beneath our station in life. Cooking is something the hired help does, not her daughter. And now I'm pregnant."

At five, Savannah's parents knocked on the door. She groaned. "Help me do this, please, Annie."

I opened the door to greet Mr. and Mrs. Charleswood. Savannah's mother had an almost regal air to her—like a queen greeting her subjects. Her two-piece suit was a pale shade of lavender and fit like it had been tailored specifically for her. Around her neck, tiny pearls lay against alabaster skin. She wore matching slingback pumps and carried a designer handbag. I could see where Savannah got her looks. Mrs. Charleswood's hair was black as night, just like Savannah's. Ice-blue eyes stared at me from beneath luxuriously long lashes. Not a frown line or wrinkle marred her classic face.

Savannah's dad embodied the essence of *GQ*. His elegantly styled silver hair matched his close-cropped beard and mustache. The charcoal suit he wore screamed money. Neither parent appeared disheveled or wrinkled after their flight and subsequent drive from the airport. I couldn't manage a short drive to the grocery store without creases and wrinkles from the seat belt. Just the thought of them entering the RV intimidated the hell out of me.

Mr. Charleswood extended his hand. "Ms. Chisholm, I'm Jeffrey Charleswood. This is my wife, Elizabeth."

"Please come in." I stepped aside, allowing them to enter. "It's nice to meet you. I wish it were under different circum-stances."

Mrs. Charleswood swept past me and spotted Savannah

on the couch. "Do you know how worried we've been, young lady?" She didn't give Savannah time to answer. "I can't believe you've been gallivanting around in"—she waved her arms around the room—"this thing. What do you have to say for yourself?"

"Elizabeth," Mr. Charleswood—Jeffrey—said. "Slow down. Give the girl a chance to talk." Jeffrey turned to me. "We do appreciate you calling. It was very kind of you to look after Savannah."

You don't even know the half of it.

Elizabeth cut him a glance that clearly said to back off. He ignored her and seated himself next to Savannah. "Are you feeling better?"

She nodded and sank lower on the couch.

"Why don't you sit," I said to Savannah's mom and pointed to the passenger seat. Anticipating their visit, I'd swiveled it around to face the living area.

"Thank you." She took a handkerchief from her purse and dusted the seat.

After serving tea, I said, "I'm going to leave the three of you alone. I'll be outside."

Savannah bolted upright. "No, don't leave."

Her mother cut her off. "Thank you, Mrs. Chisholm. We'd appreciate the privacy."

"Annie is staying." Savannah's eyes pleaded with me. "What I have to say can be said in front of her. And if you have something to say that can't be said with her in the room, then you don't need to say it."

Elizabeth Charleswood gasped. "You watch your tone."

"Whatever you want, Savannah." I plopped down in the banquette and waited.

Savannah's dad spoke first. "What's this all about? What do you have to tell us that requires an audience?"

"I'm pregnant." No preamble, no stuttering. She just

threw it out like she was announcing she was going shopping or had purchased tickets to a concert.

"What?" her mother asked, picking a piece of lint off her skirt.

"I said, I'm pregnant. I'm going to have a baby."

Mr. Charleswood's mouth opened, then closed, but Mrs. Charleswood never blinked.

"This is just a minor inconvenience. We can have it taken care of," Elizabeth said. "You can see my doctor when we get home. It's barely a procedure."

It sounded like the voice of experience, and I wondered. Savannah had said she was an only child. Sounded to me like her mother may have had a few unplanned pregnancies taken care of herself.

"My baby is not an *it*."

The tension grew palpable. Savannah's father didn't say a word, but the look in his eyes said he wasn't going to get in the middle of his wife and daughter. A situation I'd experienced with my own father. Jeffrey Charleswood may have been a powerful man, but his wife ruled the roost.

"You are hardly in a position to make this decision." Elizabeth rose and placed her cup on the counter. "Now, if you'll get your things, we need to get back to the airport."

"I'm not going anywhere." Savannah dug her heels in. "For once, you're going to listen to me."

It was Savannah's dad's turn. "Sweetheart, listen to your mother."

"Excuse me," I butted in.

Three sets of eyes turned in my direction. "Mrs. Charleswood, may I have a word with you, outside?"

She narrowed her eyes. "That won't be necessary. As soon as Savannah collects her things, we'll be leaving."

"No," I said. "I wouldn't normally get in the middle of a family matter, but I need to talk to you." I walked to the door and waited. When she didn't move, I said, "Now!"

"Very well." She followed me down the steps to the picnic table across the gravel drive. "What is it you have to say, Ms. Chisholm, that you can't say in front of my daughter and husband?"

I sat down and indicated she do the same. She hesitated but finally gave in and took a seat. "Do you love your daughter?"

She laughed. "What kind of question is that? Of course, I love Savannah."

"I mean really love her. The unconditional kind where you can see past her warts and put her needs and wants above yours."

"Savannah's a child and hardly knows what she wants. If she has this baby, within six months, she'll be off on another adventure. Two months ago, she wanted to go to culinary school, and now she wants to have a baby." She waved her hand in the air as if dismissing Savannah's dreams.

"She still wants to go to culinary school. She's a damn good cook who could be a damn good chef if given the opportunity. It means a lot to her, and so does this baby. When I first met her, she was scared and confused, but in the last several weeks, I've seen her blossom."

She tilted her head and laughed. "You've known her for, what, two or three weeks? I've known her a lifetime. Don't you dare lecture me on what is best for my child. Who do you think you are?"

I lowered my eyes and picked at a splinter on the table. "I've been in Savannah's shoes. Thirty-six years ago, I was pregnant, scared, and the only thing I wanted was my mother's love and acceptance. And she turned her back on me."

"That's where our stories differ. I'm not turning my back on Savannah."

"You are," I said. "You're turning your back on what Savannah wants. She wants this baby. You haven't even asked her about the baby's father and where he fits in the picture."

"It doesn't matter who the father is," she said. "There will be no baby."

"You really don't understand her," I said. "I feel sorry for you. She's a sweet, sensitive young lady with so much to offer, and you can't see beyond your country club mentality."

Elizabeth Charleswood stood. "I've had enough. I don't have to sit here and take your insults."

"You'll listen to me if you want to keep your daughter," I said. Tears rolled down my cheeks. "You're going to lose her, and you don't even care. If you force Savannah to have an abortion and try to press her into the mold you've created, you might as well drive off right now and leave her here. Because you will lose her. You'll break her spirit, and that's the worst thing that can happen to a person. I know from experience."

She eyed me warily but slowly sank onto the bench. "Talk."

CHAPTER THIRTY-TWO

I couldn't believe I was getting ready to tell this woman my story, but if I helped bridge a way for her and Savannah to mend their differences, then that's what I had to do. Savannah's life was going to be difficult enough, but she needed the support of her family.

"I got pregnant my senior year of college, and my mother flipped out."

"That's hardly unusual. Many—" She cleared her throat and waved her hand in a dismissive gesture. "Many girls find themselves in that careless position."

I wanted to slap her off her high horse, but Savannah's happiness was at stake. "Yes, indeed we do. Fortunately, the baby's father loved me. We got married and built a life together." Crappy as it turned out to be, at least I wasn't trying to raise a baby on my own.

She smirked. "And they all lived happily ever after."

I gritted my teeth. "No, they did not. My mother didn't speak to me for six years. And I was too stubborn to push for reconciliation."

"Save—" Elizabeth started to speak, but I cut her off.

"I'm not finished. My mother and I eventually reconciled,

but only after a horrific car crash and the death of my six-year-old son. The grandson she had never met and never wanted to meet because she was punishing me for getting pregnant." Tears welled in my eyes, but I brushed them away. I went on to tell Elizabeth all the gory details of the accident, how I walked around like a zombie for months afterward, how burying my child was the hardest thing I had ever done.

I could tell she was uncomfortable by the way she squirmed in her seat, but I pushed forward. At some point, it became less about furthering Savannah's cause and more about unburdening myself of all the massive heartache that I had carried for so long. The more the words came out, the more it felt like I was cleansing my soul. Scrubbing all the shattered parts of me and revealing the sweet tender times I'd overlooked.

"Michael must have called my parents," I said. "Because I certainly didn't. I wanted nothing to do with my mother. My father was another story—he was an innocent victim in the feud with my mother. But the day of the funeral, they showed up. I wanted more than anything to crawl into her arms and for her to comfort me, but the last words she had said were that God would punish me for getting pregnant."

Elizabeth gasped.

"What kind of person says that to their only child? I threw her words right back at her. I didn't care if I hurt her. In fact, I wanted to hurt her. Wanted to hurt her as badly as she had hurt me all those years ago. You know what? In that moment, I saw a change in her. All the hardness that had permeated my mother melted away. I don't remember who said what or how it happened, but by the time we left for the funeral, she had her arm around me, and it was . . ." I couldn't finish with the tears streaming down my face.

I felt a hand on my shoulder. When I looked up, Elizabeth handed me a tissue.

"I don't want that to happen to us," she whispered. "But she's not ready to have a baby."

I blew my nose. "That's where you come in. She's going to need all your love and support to make this happen. I believe she truly loves the baby's father. She's been talking to him."

"And he's accepted the idea of this baby."

"He doesn't know. She wanted to make sure he loved her before springing the news on him. Then she wanted to tell you."

"And does he love her?"

"Yes."

"Can he support her?" Her eyes misted.

"Only Savannah knows that, but with her passion for cooking, if she gets the opportunity to go to culinary school, I'm betting that nothing will stop them."

She nodded. "It looks like I'm going to be a . . . Dear God, I'm going to be a grandmother. I don't know if I'm ready for that."

I put my arms around her and hugged. "I think you're more than ready. Let's go talk to Savannah, shall we?"

Elizabeth went straight to Savannah and kneeled in front of the couch. "You've found a wonderful friend in Annie."

Savannah's eyes grew wide, and she shot me a questioning look. I shrugged and went to the bedroom. Far enough to be out of the way, but close enough I could hear the conversation.

"Are you sure you want this baby?"

Savannah tilted her head and placed a hand on her abdomen. "More than anything. Mom, I know I've disappointed you, but trust me on this. I know it's the right thing to do. I feel responsible for her. I mean, I know my baby may not be a her, but until I know for sure, I can't even bring myself to call her an it. She's a real person. In a little while, I'll be able to feel her move and know I've created a life."

She took her mother's hand and placed it where hers had been. "This is your grandmother, baby."

Elizabeth glanced over at Jeffrey. "Don't forget your father. He's going to be a grandfather."

Savannah's dad sat there, a smile tugging at the corner of his mouth. If he was worried about the prospect of becoming a grandfather, he didn't show it.

"What about the father?" Elizabeth asked. "Is he upstanding?"

Savannah's smile faded. "It's Seth, Mom."

Elizabeth's back went rigid. "The lawn guy?"

Savannah rose from the couch and strode across the room. "There is nothing wrong with what he does. He's saving so that he can open his own business. The important thing is that he loves me, and he makes me happy. Nothing else matters."

Savannah's dad jumped in. "She's right, Elizabeth. If he loves her and accepts this baby, what more can we ask. If the kid is serious, maybe I can help him with his business plan and get him started on the right foot."

"Would you really do that, Daddy?" Savannah asked.

"If it's that important to you, I will."

Elizabeth's shoulders drooped. "Your father's right. I'm not the one who has to live with him. You are." The ice in her voice had melted, and she sounded sincere.

Jeffrey glanced at his watch. "We need to think about getting to the airport."

I stepped back in. "Savannah doesn't need to be flying right now. The doctor said she needs to get bed rest for the next twenty-four to forty-eight hours."

"I need to get back," Jeffrey said.

"How about Savannah stays here, and if she's still doing good in a couple of days, I'll put her on a plane home." I crossed my fingers, not ready to let her go.

Savannah perked at the idea, but then said, "I need to go

back and talk to Seth."

Elizabeth patted Savannah's shoulder. "You stay here and get healthy. Seth will be there when you get home."

Savannah looked from one parent to the other. "You promise you won't say anything to him. I want him to hear about the baby from me."

Jeffrey put his arm around her and squeezed. "It's your news, sweetheart. It will hold until you get home."

"Dad, promise me you won't start talking business plans and the future with him. Don't treat him any different from how you used to treat him. In other words, ignore him. That goes double for you, Mom."

Hours after Savannah's parents had left, she and I were sitting at the table over a meal of canned soup and grilled cheese, courtesy of *moi*.

"Your cooking sucks, you know," Savannah said.

"It was this or a frozen dinner nuked in the microwave." I bit off a corner of my grilled cheese. The buttery taste was heaven to my tongue, even if the budding chef turned her nose up. "I'll have to get used to eating like this once you leave. I'm going to miss your cooking, but not as much as I'll miss you." My voice caught on the words.

"Annie, I don't know what you said to my mother, but I will be forever in your debt. If it hadn't been for you, I don't know where I'd be."

I laughed. "Sitting in some diner scheming how to ditch your check without getting caught. Or sitting along the side of the highway trying to get a trucker to give you a ride." I sobered at the thought of a pregnant Savannah hitching rides. "You're a lucky, lucky young woman."

"I'm lucky in more ways than one," she said. "Hey, where's our next stop?"

"*My* next stop is Columbia, Missouri," I said, "but we're staying here another day or two. Then I'm putting you on a plane *before* I leave."

"No fair," she said. "I can rest while you drive. What do you say, Annie? Let me make one more stop with you. Isn't that where you met Tim?"

"And Michael. Yes, it's where I went to college and Michael and Tim went to law school."

"Are you trying to downplay your conversations with Tim? I notice you two are talking a lot. Plus, you sure are texting someone a lot lately. Do you think you and Tim will get together when you get back to Florida?"

"Take a breath," I said. "Are you trying to change our conversation?" I considered her last question, though I didn't let her know. It was too soon to tell what our future held. I knew I wanted Tim in my life. I thought he felt the same, but a lot of years had passed since we were an item. I still clung to a lot of my previous baggage with Michael but was slowly coming to grips with the fact that our distance had been as much my fault as it had been his. Neither of us had found a way to move forward after losing our son.

"Are you trying to deflect my question?" Savannah asked.

"Maybe. I'm not sure what's in store for me and Tim. We'll have to figure it out. I'll have a long drive back to Florida to think about it."

A smile crossed Savannah's face. "I could come with you and then fly home. Keep you from being lonely."

"Nice try, but absolutely not. You are headed back home."

"But I can go to Columbia, right? Show me where you went to school. And where you met Tim. And Michael."

"Let me think about it."

"Okay. I'm going to take a walk and stretch my legs while you work on your article." Savannah put our plates in the sink. "I'll do those when I get back."

"But—"

"No buts. The doctor said short walks were okay."

"Go on."

Savannah stopped at the door. "Can I borrow your phone? I need to make a call, and I forgot to charge mine."

"Sure." I grabbed it off the counter and handed it to her.

Shortly after she left, I peeked out the window to check on her. She was sitting on the picnic table talking on my cell. Hopefully, she was talking to Seth and telling him she was going to head home soon. I opened my laptop and went to work.

It felt exhilarating to see the words appearing on the screen as my fingers flew across the keyboard. I hadn't had the luxury of a laptop in college and had made do with steno pads.

Thirty minutes into my writing, Savannah returned. When she saw me at the laptop, she said, "Ignore me. I'm just bringing your phone back. I'm going on my walk now."

My cell rang almost immediately after she placed it next to me. I smiled when Tim's number displayed on the screen. We *had* been talking every night.

"Hey," I answered. "I wondered if you were going to call."

"Of course. How did the visit with Savannah's parents go?"

I told him what had transpired and how Savannah's mom had a change of heart.

"I'm sorry you had to share your memories with her. I know that couldn't have been easy," he said.

I cleared my throat, fighting off the emotions that threatened to engulf me. "I didn't know any other way to get through to her."

"You're a brave woman, Annie Chisholm. Have I told you lately that I admire you?"

I smiled, my heart warming at the sound of his voice.

CHAPTER THIRTY-THREE

We stayed an extra day just to be sure that Savannah was doing okay. I caved and told her she could come with me to Columbia but only if she rested the entire way. When I was assured she was feeling better, I checked our route and chose the easiest way to Columbia, making sure we had good roads all the way. Savannah put the passenger seat all the way back and made herself a comfy nest to rest in while I drove.

Our campground in Columbia turned out to be a sterile-looking patch of ground with nary a tree in sight. We weren't far from the highway, and traffic whizzed past. I dreaded trying to sleep with all the noise. After settling in and unhooking the Jeep, I suggested a drive into town. I hadn't seen the campus since the day I graduated, and I wanted to see what had changed.

"I'm starving," I said. "I think I know where we can find a good pizza."

"Pizza sounds great," Savannah said.

The minute I walked into the restaurant, I was transported back to the night Michael and I went to the Barrister's Ball. What we didn't know was that Tim had purchased "drinks only" tickets. By the time the evening was over, Michael and I were starving. This pizza place became our favorite spot.

While Savannah perused the menu and placed our order, I scanned the restaurant, noting the changes. The travel posters depicting scenes from around Italy had been updated. Rustic wooden tables replaced the black laminated tables, which usually had cardboard coasters piled under one or more of the feet to keep them from wobbling. The best addition was a glass-front case filled with brightly colored gelatos that I couldn't wait to try.

"Hey, are you going to eat that breadstick?" Savannah pulled me back to the present.

I had been so wrapped up in my thoughts, I hadn't noticed that our food had arrived. "What?" I glanced at her hand hovering over the basket of bread. "No, go ahead."

She had already scarfed down one and snatched up the other one, which she dipped in marinara and shoved in her mouth before I could blink.

"Umm," she said, talking around the breadstick. "You were looking all moony-eyed. What were you thinking?"

A shiver crept down my spine. "Nothing, just ghosts from my past taking a stroll."

We both agreed that my favorite pizza joint still served great pizza. Savannah must have really liked it. She ate half the pie. The waitress wrapped the leftovers for a midnight snack, and we headed to the car.

"Show me the campus, okay?" Savannah clicked her seat belt and stuck her head out the window.

I slid behind the wheel and jabbed the key into the ignition. "Sure, it's grown a bit, but I think I can find my way around." The campus wasn't the only thing that had grown. I couldn't believe the traffic.

"Lots of old buildings."

"Adds to the character," I said. We drove by the Columns

—the six Ionic columns that symbolized the university—and I told her the story of how they had been around since the mid-1800s and remained after the building had been destroyed by fire. Michael, Tim, and I had spent plenty of afternoons studying on the lawn near the Columns.

Suddenly, Savannah slapped the dashboard, and I hit the brakes. "What's the matter?" I asked, my heart racing.

She smiled. "That pizza place is where you had your first date with Michael. I mean besides the ball. It's not like that was a real date, anyway. It was kind of a pity date because Tim was gone and all."

"A pity date? It was not a pity date." Not the way it turned out, it wasn't. "And yes, that's where Michael and I had our first real date, right after the ball was over."

"That's so romantic." Savannah straightened and turned to me. "Did you know then that you loved him?"

"No, I was dense in the head when it came to love. Maybe naïve is the better word," I said. "I'd never had a real relationship before. Plenty of dates, but nothing that came close to being serious."

"Poor Tim. Did you break his heart?"

"That's enough about me," I said. "Just enjoy the tour."

Savannah twisted her mouth into a pout. "You promised you'd tell me more."

"I'll get to it. We've got time. I don't want to bore you to death."

All the nostalgia surrounding my college days prompted me to ask Savannah if she would consider college if her parents let her choose.

"I don't need it," she said matter-of-factly. "My mom was a Wellesley girl and always assumed I'd trot right off and follow her legacy. But I had other plans."

I'd have given my left arm to go to Wellesley. Truly I would have. But I'd gotten the scholarship to Mizzou and the rest was history. "Have you ever wanted to do anything other than being a chef?" I asked.

"No, just culinary school. I wanted to go to Le Cordon Bleu in Paris."

"I have a good feeling about you. If you put your mind to it, you will be a total success." Arriving back at the campground, I parked the Jeep and cut the engine.

"From the time I can remember, I followed our cook around. When she baked, she'd give me bits of dough to roll out. I could make baklava before I turned six. By the time I was ten, I could make a soufflé better than hers."

"What happened?" I unlocked the door and stepped inside.

"Mother could not comprehend why any daughter of hers would want to cook—it was such a menial task." Savannah rolled her eyes. "Instead, I was supposed to spend four years getting the MRS degree so I could play tennis, host charity fundraisers, and look down on the people raising my children."

"What's an MRS degree?"

"You know, go off to school to land a rich husband and become a missus. Mrs. Vanderfluff or Mrs. Wentwhisker the Fourth."

"Isn't Wellesley an all-girls school?"

Savannah quirked an eyebrow. "It is, but they sure aren't nuns. There are colleges all over Boston. There's Harvard, MIT, Cambridge, just to name a few. That's where the old money goes."

Made sense to me. Go off to school and land a rich husband. At Mizzou, the girls in my dorm had set their sights on medical or law students. They might not be rich, but they had potential. "Tell me more about yourself."

"Like you said, we've got time. I don't want to bore you to death." She smiled. "I'm bushed. I think I'll turn in."

Touché.

Long after I'd crawled into bed, I lay awake thinking about that night with Michael. Would my life have been different if Tim's mother hadn't been sick?

CHAPTER THIRTY-FOUR

Waking before Savannah, I pulled on running clothes and slipped quietly from the RV. Last night I had purposely not driven past the park or the apartment complex where Michael and Tim had lived. Those memories were just too personal to share.

Standing in the park where it all began, I took a deep breath. The lilacs weren't in bloom, but the musty smell of fresh earth was intoxicating. My heart raced as I remembered the fragrance of the night Michael and I walked the path around the lake. I would never smell lilacs and cool, fresh earth without remembering the night Michael and I became *us*.

Shaking off the memory, I began a slow jog around the park. My muscles were stiff, and it had been years since I'd run, but somehow, being back here, it seemed right. I'd pay for my folly the next day, but running helped me focus. I rounded a bend and saw a group of young people playing football. Law students, I suspected. Though, times had sure changed. This group was almost an equal mix of male and female. Back in my day, women were in the minority at the law school.

One couple caught my eye. He was tall and lean, much like Michael. I could tell by the way they interacted that they were a couple. I also noticed a young man hanging on their every move. Something in his expression told me he was in love with the young lady.

I watched for several minutes and then headed to my car. Involuntarily, I turned the car toward Michael and Tim's apartment. I had spent as much time in the tiny townhouse as I'd spent at my own dorm, quite possibly more. When I rounded the corner, my heart skipped a beat; the old building was gone, replaced with a brick four-plex. From the looks of the grounds, it was still a party house. A rump-sprung couch graced the small patio in front of one of the units. Two trash cans overflowed with beer bottles and pizza boxes. The scene of frequent partying. I wondered if the occupants were law students or if the boundary of who lived where had been erased.

A young man exited the building, looking slightly hung over.

"Hey," I called from the car. "What happened to the row of townhouses that used to be here?"

He shrugged. Pulling a bike from behind the couch, he hopped on it and pedaled off.

Noticing an elderly woman opposite the four-plex, I let myself out of the car, crossed the street, and introduced myself. "I'm Annie Chisholm. I graduated from the university a while back."

She looked at me with tired eyes. "I think it's been more than a few years judging from the gray hair you're wearing."

I laughed. "More like a couple of decades, but I'm not counting."

"Me neither. Course, once you get my age, it doesn't matter anyway. Old is old." She pointed across the street with her broom. "And those kids make me feel older all the time. That bunch in there, destroying the place like a pack of animals. Don't see how anyone would let the rowdies take over a new place like that."

"My late husband used to live in the townhouse that was over there." I shaded my eyes against the sun and stared across the street. "I spent a lot of time there."

"Then no doubt I've seen you coming and going—probably sneaking out in the morning to get back to your dorm, huh?"

I blushed. "You lived here in the eighties?" A motorcycle roared down the street, breaking the early-morning silence. It still amazed me how quiet a college town was in the morning, especially when the days and evenings were filled with parties, barhopping, tailgating, and football games.

"My husband and I bought the place in seventy-two, right after we got married. Been living here ever since. He passed a couple years back." She crossed her wrinkled hands over the top of the broom and looked wistfully across the lawn. "He loved it here. Even with the kids across the street."

"How long has the townhouse been gone?" I asked, remembering the lilac bushes that grew on either side of the entrance. The scent had wafted into the open window the night Michael and I first made love.

"Burned down a couple of years ago. Kid passed out drunk with a lit cigarette. Place went up like someone had doused it with gasoline." She resumed her sweeping. "Idiots."

"Did he get out okay?"

"The good Lord watches over fools. Lucky for him, someone saw the flames shooting from the roof and reported it. They rescued him, but the place was too far gone. Damaged the units on both sides, so they condemned it and later tore it down. Got to be an eyesore." She cocked her head and eyed me warily. "You're the second one today who's come snooping around asking about that old townhouse."

"Probably been home to a lot of students over the years," I said.

"A real looker, he was. Had a nice butt on him too. Not that I was looking. Just because my Gerald is gone, doesn't mean I'm on the prowl. And I'm not one of those cougars you hear about. I just appreciate an attractive man when I see one. There's nothing wrong with that. Is there?"

I shook my head. "No ma'am. Nothing wrong with appreciating a nice male specimen."

"Guy was about your age."

A quiver started in my stomach. Could it be possible? "What did he look like?"

She leaned forward and winked. "You on the prowl?"

"Me? No, I was just wondering if it might be someone I went to school with."

"Well, you're not about to find out standing around here chit-chatting with me. If I were you, I'd get myself over to the park. He had on running clothes, just like you. That's where I figured he was heading." She dismissed me with a wave of her broom. "Go on. Get out of here. I've got work to do."

All the way across town, my heart pounded. I steered the car into the paved lot and got out. There were several runners jogging around the path now, all of them in pairs or pushing big-wheeled baby strollers. I scanned the area for a lone runner, but to my dismay, I didn't find one.

I headed back to the car, feeling defeated. It was nearing ten, and I still had to get Savannah to the airport to catch her flight.

Her backpack was loaded to the point of bulging, and she was staring at a pile of baby clothes lying on the sofa. "I got your note. Did you enjoy your run?"

I pulled a jug of juice from the fridge and poured a glass. "I did. You want some?"

"Nah, I'm good. I drank about a quart of milk earlier."

"Good for you. Keep your calcium level up and stay

hydrated."

"Meet anyone interesting while you were out?" Savannah's grin lit her face.

"Like?" I asked, curious at her question.

"Oh, I don't know. You probably still know a lot of people in the area." She held up the backpack. "I've shoved and smashed and practically sat on this pack and can't get another thing in it."

"I think you're changing the subject." I drained my glass and placed it in the sink.

"Not me." She pointed to the pile of baby things. "What should I do about this situation?"

"No problem." I disappeared into the bedroom and retrieved a tote bag I'd purchased along the way. "This should work."

"Excellent. I can easily get the rest in here."

I slid into the banquette and watched Savannah fold and arrange the tiny clothes. "I'm going to miss you."

"Come on, let's don't do this," she said. "You'll have me blubbering like a baby. I already can't believe I'm leaving in a few hours. Let's talk about something fun. Like your article."

"Articles." I smiled and pulled my laptop over. "What about them?"

"I want to know what they're about. You've been working on it like a madwoman. Don't I get a sneak preview?"

"It's pretty raw right now. Still needs a lot of work. Besides, I want it to be a surprise."

Savannah dropped the bag she was filling and sat next to me. She threw her arms around my neck. "Promise me we'll stay in touch, Annie. I couldn't stand it if I never saw you again."

I stroked her hair. "You know we will. We're road warriors. Once that baby gets here, you won't be able to keep me away. Your mom will be calling security when she sees me coming."

"She might. She's like that." Savannah laughed, but it was a good-natured laugh.

It made me feel good that she and her mom would have the opportunity that my mom and I didn't. If my mother had been able to get past my pregnancy and her will to control my life, we might have been friends long before Michael Junior died. And who knows? Michael and I may have been able to get past our son's death with our marriage intact. But that was a lifetime ago, and I was tired of looking back. The big windshield of Monroe's had me looking ahead more than ever before. The whole world was out there waiting for me and Savannah and Seth and the new life they had created.

I pulled away and placed my hand on her cheek. "Come on. We need to get going."

"It's way too soon, but I know I have to go. When I talked to my mom last night, she told me she made me a doctor's appointment for the day after tomorrow."

"Your mom's going to be a good grandmother," I said.

"Oh, she's already told me, she's going to be Nana instead of Grandma. But that's okay. If she's in my baby's life, I don't care what we call her."

"That's my girl," I said, squelching the moisture building behind my eyes.

Neither of us said a word on the way to the airport. We knew our time together was just about over, but we also knew we'd leave a part with the other wherever our travels took us.

"You want me to go in with you?" I said when we arrived at the departure area.

"No. This is hard enough. If you go in, I may not leave."

I reached under the seat and pulled out the tablet—the one Michael had left for me to start my adventure. "Here's some reading material for the plane," I said.

Running her hand over the cover, Savannah said, "Is this what I think it is?"

"Just a preview. It's rough. Remember that when you're

reading. Now get going before you miss your plane and I have to drive you home."

Savannah shoved the tablet into her tote and got out of the car. "I'll always remember you, Annie Chisholm." She blew a kiss. "I left a surprise for you back at the RV."

She waved and disappeared into the terminal.

I pulled into the cell phone lot and watched the planes take off. When Savannah's departure time came and went, I put the car in gear and headed back to the campground, my heart heavy with loneliness. She'd been gone less than a half hour, and I already missed her.

On the way back, I called Tim. "I put Savannah on the plane."

"You okay?" he asked.

"I will be. It's going to be an adjustment. She's been a lot of company, but she was ready to go home, and I am too." I turned onto the two-lane blacktop.

"When are you leaving?"

"I'm staying here tonight, but I'll probably get on the road tomorrow. I might stop and see Kyle since I'm so close to St. Louis."

"What about the rest of your trip?" Tim asked.

"I've seen what I needed to see."

At the next stop sign, I turned left into the campground, passed a row of cedars, and turned left again. As I neared the spot where Monroe waited, a figure sitting on the picnic table across the road caught my attention. I put the window down for a better look.

"You think you might need some company for the trip home?"

A smile spread across my face. "I think that would be just fine. Yes, I believe a traveling companion would be just the ticket."

I parked the car and the figure stood. After ending the call, I walked into Tim's arms.

CHAPTER THIRTY-FIVE

"How did you get here? When? How did you know where I was staying?" I stared into his eyes.

He glanced at his hands. "A little birdie told me."

Savannah was the only person who knew exactly where we were staying. Tim and Kaitlyn both knew we were in Columbia, but I hadn't shared the name of the campground. But how? Then I remembered Savannah borrowing my phone the day before.

"Savannah called you?"

He nodded. "Told me she was flying home today and that you might need a travel partner. I didn't think twice. Got online and booked myself a one-way flight. Like it or not, you're stuck with me, because I can't afford another last-minute ticket."

"But how? Why? Never mind, I'm just happy to see you."

He hesitated, drew in a breath, then exhaled. "A couple of months after Michael died, I wanted to call you, but I didn't know how. I had disappeared. Then when I had dealt with my grief, I realized I needed to be in your life. I needed you in my life. But it felt awkward. Like I was swooping in after you'd lost your husband, but I still had feelings for you."

"Oh, Tim." I reached across the table and put my hand over his.

"What I didn't know was if you would ever be able to trust someone with your heart again, and I didn't want to take a chance that you'd reject me. I remembered Michael's plan for your vacation. Don't ask me why it took him so long to make it up to you, but he really did try."

My throat tightened. His honesty brought out emotions I'd buried a long time ago. "That's what all those long talks in his study were about, weren't they?"

He nodded. "Michael knew he could never talk to you about it. He knew you would forgive him for being a workaholic. Who wouldn't forgive a dying man? He figured if he sent you on this trip that he'd kept putting off, it might somehow make it up to you."

"It's been an interesting journey," I said.

He smiled.

"There were things I needed to say to Michael that I wouldn't tell a dying man, and probably would never say out loud if I had stayed isolated in my house. But on the road, it's different. There's freedom. What I didn't count on was Savannah, and what a blessing she was. I probably would have turned back when Kyle showed up. But Savannah gave me the strength to keep going. She scared me, but she was a light that kept burning and urging me forward."

"If you had turned back, we would have never found each other," Tim said. "You needed this time to parse your grief."

"I feel like I can move forward." I rubbed my fingers over his hand. "My heart is open, and I'm willing to take a chance, if you are."

Tim's arms circled me. "Annie, I know I've let you down, but I will always be there for you. There's no one I'd rather take a chance on."

In his eyes, I saw the friend that Tim had always been to Michael and to me. Why I'd never seen his love for me was something I couldn't fathom. How different my life might have been if I had gone to the Barrister's Ball with Tim instead of Michael. How different it might have been if anything had changed, really.

Tim tilted my chin. "I know I've dumped a lot of heavy stuff on you. What's on your mind? I can see it in your eyes."

"Maybe regrets and what-should-have-beens."

He locked eyes with me. "Don't have regrets. Things happen for a reason. Who knows where we'd be if things had gone differently? But I do know where we are now, and I can see a whole future ahead of us. Just you and me growing old together."

I laughed. "If you haven't noticed, I'd say the old part is already here."

With that, Tim pressed his lips against mine. My knees trembled, and I felt like a schoolgirl again—all aflutter. I wanted to write his name on my notebook and draw hearts around our initials. I felt myself falling for a man I'd known almost all my life, and he felt the same way.

When Tim finally drew away, he said, "Annie Chisholm, I want to spend the rest of my life with you."

"You do know the right things to say, don't you."

When we hit the road, this time Tim was in the driver's seat, and I was proud to be sitting right alongside him. Michael was still with us in both our hearts and in the urn. I still planned to spread his ashes over our son's grave. But with Tim by my side. I thought Michael would approve.

I hoped the trip to Florida would be a slow one. We had a lot of time to make up, many sunrises to watch, and an open road ahead of us.

EPILOGUE

My life, for as long as I could remember, had been a petri dish teeming with *what-I-should-have-dones, what-I-wanted-to-dos,* and *what-I-dids,* until Friday, May 28. That was the day I opened the door to my heart.

Today when the doorbell rang, I opened it and saw my husband standing there with an armload of magazines.

"Why didn't you use your key?" I asked.

"As you can see, my arms are full."

"Is that what I think it is?" I grabbed one off the stack. On the cover was a photo of me standing next to Monroe in my mother's front yard.

"Bought every one at the market," Tim said. "The guy thought I was nuts until I showed him my wife on the cover. Figured you'd want to send one to each of your kids."

"Yes, and one to Savannah too." I flipped through the pages until I found my first of many articles, and there was my byline.

"Notice anything else?" Tim angled his head toward the driveway. "Thought you might like a first look at our ride for the summer."

I couldn't believe my eyes. "Is that what I think it is?" I

ran down the sidewalk. "Is this really Monroe? Did you lease Monroe for the entire summer?"

Tim joined me and opened the door. "It is definitely Monroe, but I didn't lease it. I bought it. What better way to celebrate my retirement and you starting your novel than to spend the summer in the very RV that brought us together."

I slid my arm around him and kissed his cheek. "I can't believe you did this."

He grabbed my hand and pulled me inside. "I've got something to show you."

On the table was a box of envelopes. "How did you pull this off without me knowing about it?"

He put his finger to my lips. "Woman, you talk too much."

I kissed him again.

He wrapped one arm around my waist and reached around me to pull an envelope from the box. "Are you at all interested in our first stop?"

"Not only am I interested in our first stop, but I'm also interested in all of our stops." I pulled the envelope from his hand and tore it open. Three items slid onto the table: a photo, a map, and a letter. The letter was addressed to me, and I recognized the handwriting. My hands shook as I unfolded it.

Dear Annie,

I miss you. It's hard to believe so much has happened since you found me stowed away on Monroe. My life is richer for having met you. Little Annie is growing like a weed. She'll be six months old next week. Not a day goes by that I don't vow to be a good mother to her. She's such a blessing, and I am very lucky.

Seth's business is starting to take off. My dad helped him with his business plan like he promised. Dad provided the start-up money, and Seth accepted on the condition that it was an investment. Obviously, Mom and Dad were his first customers, but with Dad's connections, it won't be long before Seth has to hire additional help. My father has even taken on the role of silent partner, though Mom and I did catch him on one of the lawn mowers the other day. I

NEVER thought I'd see my dad mowing grass, but he says if he's going to invest in a business, he needs to know how it operates. HA! We think he just likes playing with boy toys. And believe it or not, he and Seth have found they share a common interest or two. They both love baseball and beer. Finally, Dad will have someone to share his season tickets with.

My mom and I are getting along good. She's a great Nana and even babysits Annie occasionally. Seth and I have talked about me going to culinary school. It won't be Le Cordon Bleu in Paris but believe it or not they have a school in Boston. How exciting is that? I'll wait until Annie's older, maybe even when she's in school, but just knowing that I can have my family and follow my dream is too good to be true.

How are you and Tim doing? Sorry we couldn't make it to the wedding, but when Annie decided to arrive on Christmas Day, there was no way we could make your New Year's Eve ceremony. Thanks for the pictures. You looked beautiful, and you guys make a great-looking couple. Little did I know that day in Columbia when I snuck behind your back and called him that the two of you would wind up married.

Tim called the other day and said he was buying Monroe, and you were getting ready for a big road trip. You know Mom and Dad's big circular driveway is perfect for Monroe. Me, Seth, and the baby are just out back in the guest house.

Mom asks about you often and will be glad to see you. I was sorry to hear about your mother's passing and will forever be in her debt for her talk—even though she embarrassed the stuffing out of me. It was just what I needed to be able to get the courage to talk to my mom. We are so thankful to you for getting us to a place where we could communicate.

I can't wait for you to get here and meet your namesake. She has her daddy's smile and my dark hair. Counting the days . . .

All my love,
Savannah

The photo was of Seth, Savannah, and baby Annie—all

wearing white shirts and blue jeans, and the map had Boston circled.

"Oh, what a wonderful surprise! I can't wait for you to meet Savannah. You'll love her just as much as I do. And I can't wait to meet Seth and Annie. I may never want to come home."

Tim smiled and put his arm around me. "Slow down. You're talking a mile a minute."

I slid my hand over the rest of the envelopes. "Where else are we going?" I pulled another envelope out and started to open it, but Tim grabbed it from my hand.

"No peeking. It will spoil all the surprises I have waiting for you." He tucked the envelope back into the box and then laced his fingers through mine.

Photo Credit: Alecia Hoyt

Tricia L. Sanders writes cozy mysteries and women's fiction with a dash of romance and a sprinkling of snark to raise the stakes. Her heroines are humorous women embarking on journeys of self-discovery all the while doing so with class and sass.

Tricia is a recent transplant to Texas, but she's still an avid St. Louis Cardinals baseball fan, so don't get between her and the television when a game is on.

A former instructional designer and corporate trainer, she

traded in curriculum writing for novel writing, because she hates bullet points and loves to make stuff up. And fiction is more fun than training guides and lesson plans.

facebook.com/authortricialsanders

amazon.com/stores/Tricia-L.-Sanders/author/B076NXMMFW

bookbub.com/profile/tricia-l-sanders

ALSO BY TRICIA L. SANDERS

Grime Pays Mystery Series

Murder is a Dirty Business

Between hot flashes and divorce papers, a middle-aged woman reconsiders her outlook on life when she butts heads with a hot detective during a murder investigation.

Death, Diamonds, and Freezer Burn

An unwelcome visitor, an unrequited love, and a dead body create chaos in Cece's plan for a productive summer.

Pensions, Tensions, and Homicide

A former friend, a runaway mother, and a dead body threaten to spoil Cece's low-key family Thanksgiving.

Mimosas, Magnolias, and Murder

Cece wants a day of self-care, mother-daughter time…and anything but her ex-husband's wedding.

The Mattie and Mo Mysteries

Hark! A Homicide (Prequel)

When a dead elf threatens to spoil Pine Grove's Christmas, being on Santa's naughty list is the least of Mattie's worries.

Flea Market Felony

These new retirees have just hit the road. Will their first campsite's shenanigans land them both in handcuffs?

www.ingramcontent.com/pod-product-compliance
Lightning Source LLC
Chambersburg PA
CBHW072008210726
48294CB00013B/1720